The Walking Trip

Other Books by Henrietta Buckmaster

N O V E L S

The Lion in the Stone

All the Living

And Walk in Love

Bread from Heaven

Fire in the Heart

Deep River

H I S T O R Y

Let My People Go:
A History of the Anti-Slavery Movement

Freedom Bound: Reconstruction, 1865–1877

B I O G R A P H Y

Paul: A Man Who Changed the World

The Walking Trip

HENRIETTA BUCKMASTER

Harcourt Brace Jovanovich, Inc., New York

First edition

ISBN 0-15-194189-0

Library of Congress Catalog Card Number: 73-182324

Printed in the United States of America

A B C D E

For Freda
so she can reach the end

The Walking Trip

The First Day

Fasten your seat belt flashed on and Maddy Sayer fumbled for the buckle as she peered out over the houses and fields of England. Two weeks ago England had been a red shape on the map, as far away as China. In a brief delicious panic she wondered if Richard would recognize her after four years. At fifteen she probably looked older than she did now at nineteen, because at fifteen she was trying to look twenty-five.

The plane touched the runway and rolled toward the terminal. The woman sitting next to her asked if she would get down her coat from the overhead compartment and Maddy stood on the seat to oblige.

"Well, I hope you enjoy yourself," the woman said as Maddy helped her on with the coat. "I do say for a fact there's no place like home—though it's my home, not yours, isn't it?" Her soft face looked astonished for a moment. "Well, never mind."

Maddy said, "It looks good," as she slung her bulging old pouch over her shoulder. "I guess I'll get a taste for new places."

She inched down the aisle, stooping for glimpses out of each window so that the man behind her trod on her heels and apologized with a start.

There was a long wait in the cavernous baggage room and she held a slow converse with a red-bibbed porter who had voted Labour for thirty years. When the treadmill began delivering its treasures, she plucked off her single bag, shook hands with the porter and went to the customs.

She was waved through before she had a chance to study the faces beyond the barrier. She walked toward that amorphous cloud of self-conscious friends and relatives so that Richard would have plenty of time to spot her. Then she stood for some time examining each young man just in case Richard and she had been looking in opposite directions.

A young man with nothing special about him except his cold eyes and his carefully and expensively trimmed long hair examined her with equal attention from behind the barrier, frowning a bit. He had already had a word with a flight stewardess. "Could you tell me what Madeline Sayer looks like? I'm supposed to meet her since her brother can't come."

"About my size," the stewardess had said. "Size three dress, five-two, hundred pounds, cropped curly hair, blond." The vital statistics had tripped out winningly because they reflected, not adversely, on the stewardess's own charms.

The young man had opened his cold eyes wide and then closed them appreciatively. "Thanks!"

A five-foot-two female with cropped blond hair revolved slowly, as though looking for someone, not ten feet away. As Madeline passed him he looked sharply at her suitcase. "M.S." was stamped in gold on the blue cloth.

No Richard, she thought. He had not said he would meet her. An airport was an airport. The next move was to get into London.

"How do I get into London, please?" she asked a porter, and he showed her where the airline bus was waiting.

The young man was right behind her. With skill and some dash he made sure that she moved toward two empty seats in the rear. He was brisk, bright and chatty and created a realistic impression of a young man at no pains to hide his interest in this world of contained bedlam and pretty girls. Even before the bus started he told her that he had just got off a flight from Cape Town and she told him she came from the United States.

"First trip?"

She nodded and said, "Cape Town! My brother Richard came in from Lusaka, Zambia, the other day."

"That's right in our bailiwick. What's he doing down there?"

"Some kind of aid program."

"You meeting him?" His eyes were fixed on her face, his raincoat huddled in his arms.

"Yes. We're going on a walking trip in Scotland."

"Good! I hope you enjoy it. Well, take a look. What do you think of London?"

When they pulled into the terminal he waited politely for her to go ahead of him down the aisle and they stood in a little stockade of his two cases, filled at the last moment with odds and ends to give weight, and her suitcase marked with the gold letters.

She looked around for Richard. Just for a moment the world seemed very strange. A porter with grey sideburns, a large morose nose and sad eyes that had looked on much confused baggage said, Yes, anyone waiting for passengers from Flights 707, 233 or 543 would be standing right here.

No Richard.

She consulted a cable folded into her passport. "I'm going to the Chesterton Place Hotel, Spence Street, SW3."

"That would be a taxi, miss."

5

The young man said, "Cromwell Road?"

"Right out the main entrance, sir."

Maddy said to the young man, "Well, good luck." He replied, "Good luck to you. Bye-bye."

He waited till he saw her get into a taxi, then took a small book from his pocket and wrote down her address.

The Chesterton Place Hotel was the kind of small private hostelry that is found in old cities. There was no lobby to speak of, merely a wide corridor with one or two leather chairs facing the desk where a clerk reigned. The clerk was nondescript except for his taste: he brushed his hair low over his forehead and wore sideburns that met his mustaches. But these details seemed to bear little relation to his *persona.*

Maddy said, "My name's Madeline Sayer. My brother's reserved a room for me."

The clerk engaged in a brief consultation with a file. "Room twenty-six. Please sign this registration card."

She did as she was told, picked up the key and said, "Is my brother in the hotel now?"

"Brother?"

"Richard Sayer."

"Oh. Oh, I see. Oh, yes, your reservation *was* made by a Richard Sayer. By cable." He produced a form. "For the twelfth. And a reservation for himself on the tenth." He looked at her with opaque eyes. "No one claimed that reservation. On the tenth."

She took the cable from him but it yielded no more than he said. She made a small grimace of wonder. "Funny. But he's meeting me today. You'll have a room for him, won't you?"

"Well—"

"Please. He'll be here. Thanks very much."

"The lift's to your left."

6

Room 26 had once attempted to develop character but time and new chintzes had muddled its point of view. Maddy glanced around and thought it looked like a place the family stayed at in Rockport, Maine. She went to the window before she unpacked, an old habit, and liked what she saw. Small streets. A store across the way with mullioned windows. A pearly sky. A boy on a motorbike. A pigeon who sat on an outcropping of stone and made polite conversation. All familiar, yet—she drew a deep breath—London, not Boston. She liked that.

She had carried placards for peace, Bobby Seale, Angela Davis. Every Saturday morning, between classes, she passed out antipollution leaflets in front of the supermarket. She wanted everyone to have a good life and she had no hang-ups about it. Now it was time she saw the world.

But where was Richard to show it to her? A moment's unease passed over her like a shadow. She shook herself and sniffed the carbon monoxide expertly. Much better than Boston. Was she becoming an Anglophile? She laughed and drew in her head.

Unpacking her bag she thought how lucky she was. London was just a beginning. She had large expectations. She intended to make Richard look at them all so that they could decide just which direction her life should go.

After she had unpacked and put away her bag and changed her dress, she felt prickles, like a flock of small birds, walk down her spine. Richard was an idiot. Did he think she had all the time in the world? She unstuffed some of her shoulder bag, took her key and went out to explore.

Standing at the corner of Spence Street where it crossed something else, she looked around her with pleasure. The low houses, the clean streets—O Boston!

She went down one street and up another, looking at everything, seeing with wonderfully fresh and candid eyes. She bought a map and chatted with the storekeeper. He showed that he enjoyed talking to her, a small, bright, pretty and eager American.

She bought a picture postcard of Westminster Abbey and sent it to the family. She walked along Sloane Street and took her time in front of the windows. Old silver was not her specialty but she stared into a window of heavy tea services because, in the glass, she saw London moving behind her. She sensed that you must make yourself understand why the place where you stand is wondrously new— why no one had ever stood here before in exactly this way —because at nineteen you sometimes take too much for granted, especially if you are happy and things are going your way.

She moved along in the sunlight and listened to voices and looked into faces. *What do I want?* Everything.

By midafternoon she was sitting in Hyde Park by the Serpentine talking to a man with a supply of crumbs for the pigeons. He was not very responsive until he discovered that she liked pigeons. Then he turned shy grey eyes on her and found another bag of crumbs for her. This loosened his tongue.

When she had used up the crumbs she played ball with a silent eight-year-old until the man said they were bothering the pigeons. Then the eight-year-old sat on the bench and talked thoughtfully about feathered friends.

At five thirty she jumped up in dismay and looked around for a telephone. The little boy offered to conduct her and bounced his ball to the red box, asking slow penetrating questions about America.

The hotel had no message. Richard had neither arrived nor telephoned.

"What's happened to him?" the child asked.

"Maybe he forgot I was coming today," she answered lightly.

He resumed the bouncing. "Do you forget things?"

"Everyone does." Though in her heart she did not believe Richard ever forgot important things.

"I forgot my cousin's birthday party once."

"Oh. Tough luck. Where's Sloane Street?"

"Right past that statue of everyone chasing that dog."

He watched after her for a few minutes, bouncing the ball so expertly that he scarcely needed to look at it.

She was not returning to the hotel. She had simply felt the need to get moving, find her bearings, not be disappointed. Going the length of Sloane Street again, she looked at people and liked the way they walked, not tearing along, or tearing along in a different way. She stood against the Cadogan Square railings, observing. She observed for maybe ten minutes. Finally, turning her face to the sun, she found she was glad she was a girl, pleased that she could not imagine being bored, thankful that the unexpected was always happening and she was not afraid. That was a big step. Sometimes you acted cocky and did a put-on because you had too much imagination and things happened out of context.

But did they? She almost thought they did *not* happen out of context and, in the last few weeks, she had been gathering together some workable rules. When she got to Sloane Square, she turned down King's Road because it looked as though it belonged to her generation.

The stores were a nice mix. An antique store with Georgian candlesticks and Crown Derby plates in the window had no problem living next to ABANDON HOPE, a small crowded shop with its name written in smeared red letters on a window of junk and fantastic clothes. A thing called The American Drugstore had corner windows cluttered with objects of the neon fake-culture and it held her entranced for five minutes. Even a supermarket managed to combine an American *zeitgeist* with King's Road affability, and she wandered about looking at the shelves. On the street again,

9

she smiled at a lady with a Pekinese. The lady nodded. Although magentas and greens and oranges swept over King's Road, sober little shops that had served sober little people for a long time balanced the whole with equanimity.

Batik trousers, the beginning or the end of a fad, very short miniskirts, camp dresses drooping to the ankles, long hair and beards on the youths, long or cropped hair on the girls kept saying to her *It's all one. The world's of a piece.* At the same time, the middle-aged matrons with dogs did not seem out of place, and the square businessmen with briefcases pursued business with no sign of being *outré.*

When she felt hungry she looked about for a place to eat. The Chelsea Pantry. It was crowded. A waitress-student with long hair scraped back, skirts to her thighs and a laden tray indicated with her elbow a vacant chair at a table otherwise occupied.

Maddy nodded to the three who sat at the table and they made a reserved acknowledgment. Not unlike the College Appletree in Rutland, Vermont.

But after a time she sensed a difference. She longed to talk but there was no give. The three were very cool. . . . Her own age . . . no, older . . . though the red-haired, red-mustached youth could not be more than twenty-one. The small, thin-faced, long-haired girl wore a wedding ring and an Indian headband and belonged, by a mysterious but sure linkage, to the bearded third who had a silk scarf knotted inside his chamois jacket. He was the one who glanced at Maddy once or twice out of dark eyes and then looked away at his hands, which were cajoling the silver lining of an empty cigarette package into an ornament. Very deft. She watched. He glanced at her again and added a twist of yellow foil from the ashtray. Very beautiful. Now she smiled openly for this was a good language to exchange. But he turned away. The girl with the wedding band smiled, though briefly, showing large teeth in a large mouth in a thin little face.

Maddy looked at her bill. She had not the slightest idea how the pence corresponded to the coins in her pocket. She held out a ten-shilling piece to the girl and said, "How much is this?" After that the three became four by an unspoken but understood ritual of group rearrangement.

American? The cool eyes all studied her for a moment. George of the beard said he was anti-American. His announcement was courteous and carried no more stress than would a similar announcement about runner beans. But Sandra was inclined to be sympathetic to Americans; it must be difficult, being so big and so troubled.

Norman (or so they called him; no one was introduced) had weightier opinions but in struggling with them he said nothing, merely looked at her intently and raised his brows.

They sat together for an hour. Though the restaurant was crowded, no one asked them to leave. They bought coffee and someone (who was greeted briefly as Hector) crowded in with a chair and ate a silent dinner, departing with a nod.

Maddy asked questions. The answers were sometimes more oblique than she would have gotten at home but she was quick to follow up clues. Mod films, for example. They knew more about this underground world—names, techniques, styles—than she did, but she held her own well enough. They all knew pretty much what they wanted out of a crazy society, but a listening ear would have found it all rather tribal, drums patted and signals sent out, totems venerated, a sort of telepathy relied on more than speech. Norman was especially good at this telepathy, not saying much but making her understand perfectly. He was kind also. He took the last cookie but he broke it in half and shared it with her.

They seemed anxious not to appear too serious or too explicit, and she could play this as lightly as they. They were susceptible to the same currents, like birds not moving their wings but going where they intended.

Maddy found that the boys were not interested in social problems, only in life.

"They stand on the edge of rallies," Sandra said affectionately, "and turn their backs. I don't. They're pro-Soviet because they're anti-American. I'm not. But I fancy being what we are is what we want."

What we are is what we want. That was the language Maddy trusted. She knew her way confidently through its syntax. Although she spoke American and they spoke English, they shared a deeper language and they knew what they were exchanging without interpretation. They were as ego-centered as she and their responses were as spontaneous as hers when some sharp color in life, or some nuance, became important.

Well, she was glad she had found them. They came out together into the late twilight. The three were mates, and they had opened up a little and included her; though, as George said with a glint, "You're American and you're a bit too straight."

"I'm not!" she said, her large brown eyes indignant.

"Have you ever *been* anywhere?" he asked sternly, looking down at her with a frown.

"Like where?"

"Spain . . ."

Sandra giggled. "We got to Spain just last year."

Maddy said, "I've never been any place. But I'm here now."

They walked with her to where Spence Street came into King's Road. She said she was meeting her brother. Their goodbyes were casual. If they met again they would pick up exactly where they had left off.

She ran up the hotel steps and said to the new clerk at the desk, "My brother, Richard Sayer—has he come?"

"No, miss."

She was dismayed. "He must have come!"

"There's no one registered by that name, miss."

"A message?"

"No, miss."

She was suddenly empty and confused. She went to the street door, but the street was unfriendly, the twilight had turned into night. She looked at the narrow lobby, at its chairs with their indented leather cushions, reminders of all the uneasy rumps which had pressed them out of shape, at the unemptied ashtrays; above all, she was assailed by the dead air, which, at that moment, became intolerable.

The lift was a cell. She struck it with the back of her hand and danced with impatience until she could burst through the door.

Yet she was more indignant than apprehensive. Richard had come six thousand miles from Zambia and then couldn't find the hotel!

Perhaps he had cabled home. But Mom knew where she was and would let her know.

On the tenth . . . He had not picked up his reservation on the tenth.

Yet his second cable to her was dated London, May 10.

Second cable . . . She shook out her bag, disgorging two cables and two letters, along with a mini radio and a book. Taking off her shoes and propping herself on the bed, she laid the two letters and two cables beside her and read the second cable first.

WILL IN MIDDLESEX BANK CHAMBERS STREET ACCESS MADELINE RICHARD SAYER ONLY.

"Will who?" her roommate had asked, giggling.

She had not given the cable proper attention until she was on the plane. Then she had thought, "Wills. I suppose that's what they teach you in the Peace Corps and if you work for Arthur D. Short, Inc. To look ahead. Who's going to die?"

Now she studied the cable carefully, trying not to miss

13

a nuance. When she put it down all the substance she had gleaned was the address of the Middlesex Bank, which she might need if Richard did not show up in the morning.

But people did not just disappear! They went off to live their own lives and they reappeared when they were ready. Her generation anyway . . . But a respectable young businessman who had invited his only sister to come three thousand miles, would he just disappear without giving her a thought?

Don't answer that!

Due on the tenth. He was nearly three days late.

Don't think about that!

She sensed that facts were confusing; she needed to know something else, something not written down. Her mother—she trusted her mother almost as much as she trusted Richard. For a wild moment she thought of calling home and saying, "Mom dear, what do you make of all this? Exactly what kind of a job did Richard have in Zambia? Did you know his wife had left him?"

But Maddy could not do that. She had quit running home at the first sign of confusion. Besides, Richard had said in his first letter: "This must be hugged to your bosom until I allow you to speak."

To the comforting roar of the King's Road traffic and the occasional voice and slammed car door of Spence Street, she read the first letter slowly, looking between these lines as well.

"Dear Sibling. Do you still love and remember me? I wish I hadn't been such a wretched correspondent but, in my innocence, I thought I could manage the world and a wife. Humbling is the word. Incidentally, this letter is private. What I want of you and what I want to tell you must be hugged to your bosom until I allow you to speak. Agreed?

"What I want to tell you is that Cloris has left me. It's been a bad blow. I realize that none of you ever met her,

14

but I loved her—I love her. Her reasons seem terribly strong and I agree that my way of life makes marriage difficult—but I don't know how to change. This Africa is like my soul to me. I sin against Africa and so against myself. Cloris doesn't understand. I don't blame her. I admit it's a sort of Holy Grail attitude. If you make the commitment it does not leave you alone.

"I can't sort out things here. The emotional climate, the mystique, if you like, the pull, the drag, the soaring, the heat, the demands never leave you alone. Cloris was right that I can't even see myself any more or hear my own voice. I'm due for a leave. What I want from you is this: meet me in London and go with me into the wild wilds of Scotland. Will you? I'll pay all your expenses. Will you? I need someone I love and trust, who has good sense, who knows how to wear a knapsack and keep her mouth shut and walk twenty miles a day to help me through this Gehenna. You're the only one. I know it means cutting classes but you're too bright anyway. Will you? Will you? Bring your guitar if you want. *I'll* carry it. But cable Yes like a good girl. Love, Dickon X."

She had, that day, cabled YES. It was a foregone conclusion. Signing himself Dickon, the name she had called him as a child, sealing memories with "X," their code for secrecy when she was in the eighth grade and he in college, was recalling the brother without equal who had taken her on adventures, listened to the confusion of her adolescence, offered remedies, offered insights, offered faith, kicked open doors.

Maddy had never really wanted to see a picture of Cloris —she had glanced at the wedding picture sent home and made a weak joke—because she could not imagine any wife worthy of him.

Cloris had made him unhappy. Somehow it was Cloris's fault that he had let down Maddy today.

Well, goodbye Cloris.

She looked at the first cable again, with the address of the hotel, to make sure that it had been sent from Lusaka. *Lusaka, Zambia.*

She folded the two cables and the first letter and stared at them coolly. She read the second letter which had carried his check.

"Good Old Short Hair. Bless you. You signed a new lease on life for me. There's more money where this came from. Let me know your flight and I'll try to meet you, though I won't promise. I'll cable as soon as I know where we have reservations in London. You can tell Mother and Father now that you're meeting me—but still don't mention Cloris. You can give them this itinerary. We'll get out of London in twenty-four hours. Stay a couple of days in Edinburgh: Mount Royal Hotel, Princes Street, then take the train for Inverness: Station Hotel. Inverness is a jewel but we'll polish it only long enough to pick up some camping equipment and rent a car. I did say *hiking* and I mentioned twenty miles—but starting from a car! I hope that doesn't shock you. I haven't really become effete; I'm merely looking for options. Do you remember when I went to the north of Scotland before? Well, perhaps you don't. You had a boy friend that spring and couldn't think of anything else. Sutherland and Wester Ross are—with Africa!—my land forever. It's the loneliest land I can imagine and yet it's grand and living. It needs no one and in fact there is no one. Twenty miles without a croft. The moors are as mysterious as the desert. They make the same sort of demand. In the west are granite glens formidable and chilling, yet the earth around them is alive with peat cuttings. When you come down into Tongue, at the very top of Scotland (we'll stay there for a few days at the hotel) the sea is as blue as the Mediterranean. That's enough from me. Take a map. Do your own work. Find Inverness, Lairg, Tongue, Ullapool and try to imagine what goes on in between.

"On the twelfth day of May in London I'll greet you without a smile and say gruffly, 'Well, you certainly took your own time to get here. . . .'

"Darling Maddy, thank you with all my heart!"

She suddenly crumpled the letter. *Oh, Richard, it's you who are taking your own time!* She said aloud, "Richard would *not* freak out! Richard would *not* let me down. I know what I know!"

She walked around the little room, standing for a long time at the dark window.

She had never, in her whole life, been in a strange place without friends.

What if he's been in an accident! The police would look in his pockets and what would they do? Cable Zambia.

Maddy, go to the police!

But if she went to the police at this time it would mean she was scared, and she was not scared.

Had he actually arrived in London?

The last cable had been dated "London." Was that enough to go on?

A very faint chill crept over her. Not enough to induce fright but enough to send up a small fluttering signal that might become alarm.

The Second Day

When she wakened in the morning she knew that something uneasy had grown in her consciousness during the night. She identified it in the morning light as Richard's second cable: "WILL IN MIDDLESEX BANK . . . ACCESS MADELINE RICHARD SAYER. . . ."

Will—why? What was he saying to her by *will*?

She seldom conceded that lack of experience stood in her way but she was honest enough to recognize ignorance. Did he mean something by *will*?

She dressed in a tearing hurry, asking but not answering questions. As she drew a comb through her hair and put some blue around her eyes, she stopped suddenly. Panic, Madeline, and you'll run right up the wall. Go to the bank quietly. Be cool. Use your head. He's got a reason. Are you scared? No!

Breakfast came on a tray. She set to it gratefully. Eat calmly!

After breakfast she disposed of his arrival at London Airport. This took patience and a long wait on the telephone and an irascible supervisor, but in time she had the hard fact that Richard Sayer had been checked onto Flight 710, May 9, at Lusaka, which flight had arrived ten minutes late in London on the tenth.

The hotel clerk had no message for her except that he could no longer hold Mr. Sayer's reservation. She said, "All right. We'll find some place else."

At the bank she was greeted with great satisfaction because her signature was needed to reinforce Richard's directions. She wrote her name with an odd relief, as though pieces of a puzzle were coming together, for just above her signature was Richard's handwriting, as clear as though carved in stone: "Richard Sayer, Lusaka, Zambia." And the date, May 10. London address? American Embassy.

"Why did he give the American Embassy?" she asked the brushed, middle-aged banker with immaculate spectacles as he handed her the key to the deedbox.

He looked at the address. "He said he would be in London only till you arrived."

"He said that? Those were his words? *You* spoke to him?"

The spectacles were surprised. "I did."

"You see, we were to meet yesterday but he wasn't there. He made a reservation for himself at the hotel but he did not pick it up. I haven't heard a word."

"Oh . . . well . . . I daresay—"

"I would like to see what's in this box."

The spectacles glinted. "An emergency—his instructions are quite clear. Only an emergency. We can't go beyond his instructions. There is no emergency. You would see that."

Her large brown eyes came to rest on his face. He did not believe in an emergency. She did not want to believe in an emergency. She stood up. "I guess I should go to the embassy too."

"That's very wise, Miss Sayer. It's a good thing for nationals to register at their embassy. If he gave the embassy as his address then he has registered there. Thank you very much."

She was put smoothly onto the street with directions for Grosvenor Square.

The embassy was full of Americans. When she said she wished to register she was given a form. As she handed it back to the clerk she said, "My brother gave the embassy as his London address. Did he have to fill out a form like this?"

"Certainly."

"May I see it?"

"I'll verify." The girl spoke with a Maltese accent and came back to say Mr. Sayer had not registered.

Maddy received this news as she leaned against the counter, gripping her old shoulder bag. Between the bank and the embassy—and the hotel—what had happened? Suddenly she needed help. She knew it as realistically as the fact that she was leaning against the hard edge of a piece of furniture.

Within five minutes she was facing a vice-consul of about Richard's age.

"He went to the bank but he did not come to the embassy. He did not pick up his hotel reservation. I haven't heard a word. It's not like him. Absolutely *unlike* him."

The vice-consul read the two cables and handed them back without comment. "He gave the embassy as his address? I'll check again." He was gone for five minutes.

"No, he did not register, but I shouldn't worry. These things happen all the time. What was your brother's job?"

She hesitated and then she made a little grimace. "With one of those research and reconstruction outfits—Arthur D. Short, Inc.? Would that be right? My father said they handled a million things and I never figured out where Richard fitted in."

Whether he was writing or making chicken tracks, she

did not know. He glanced at her. "Arthur D. Short, Inc., feasibility studies, industrial research and advice to developing countries? Then I certainly shouldn't worry about him. It's only twenty-four hours. Though we can check the hospitals if you like."

"Please!"

"Give me your telephone number and I'll get in touch with you."

"Do it now, please!"

"Miss Sayer, it's the lunch hour. I'm not sure I can get the information."

"Please. Now."

He studied her for a moment and surrendered.

"Good morning. This is the American Embassy. I am inquiring for an unidentified male brought in within the last three days. Yes, I'll hold on. . . . Thank you. . . . Good morning. This is the American Embassy. I am inquiring . . . Twenty-seven years old. Sandy hair. Five-ten. Oh, thank you. . . ." As he dialed again, he said to her, "Forty years old, black hair, six-two."

She smiled faintly. "What if something happened outside London?"

"Please don't get nervous. Really, you have no idea how often the most conventional people lose all sense of time."

She merely stirred; she did not get up.

"He may not care to have questions asked about him so soon."

"He wouldn't let me down," she said.

"You haven't seen him, you say, for four years."

"He's my brother."

He said gently, "He sounds to me like a man who can look after himself. Something very explainable has happened. Give it one more day. And then remember we're here to help. It would be easier for us to handle inquiries than you."

21

"Why?"

"Well, that's one of our reasons for being here, isn't it? You have friends in London?"

"No."

"Your brother must have friends."

"I don't know who they are. His wife lives here." She was amazed at the words. They came out of her mouth as unexpectedly as a chain of paper dolls. All she could think was that she was putting cards on the table and, without real volition, asking for help.

"His wife! You mean he has a wife?"

"Separated from her."

"Recently?"

She nodded wretchedly as though she had broken a confidence.

"Well then, I certainly shouldn't worry. This is probably the answer. . . . He's with his wife again and you may not hear for a while. . . . But do please remember we have very direct concern for any Americans in difficulties. . . ."

She studied the Roosevelt statue in Grosvenor Square for some minutes. Is that it? Richard with Cloris? Of course. Damn him.

She was surprised that she had not thought of this herself. As she kicked the toe of her shoe against the base of the statue, it seemed more and more likely. He got in on the tenth, he went to the bank, then his unhappiness about Cloris got the better of him and he called her. Cloris was as unhappy as he, they fell into each other's arms, goodbye, Maddy.

She kicked at the paving. She looked at the golden eagle over the embassy and hated every feather and claw. If he is lost with Cloris he will reappear when he chooses. . . . But not a message . . . not even the smallest message whispered over Cloris's telephone.

The vice-consul had suggested that people changed in four years.

That did not feel right. She held onto something terribly amorphous. At the same time she asked herself a hard question: did she simply not want to believe that Richard had changed? Or even that Richard was married. *That* went very deep.

The streets were her friends. Enclosures would have driven her mad. Never in her whole life had she wanted to be fooled. She did not want to be fooled now by any wishful thinking or tired aphorisms or false hopes.

She walked doggedly until she had convinced herself that she was willing to face the truth even if it came as a blinding disillusion. Only then was she able to go back to the hotel.

"My brother? Any messages?"

The clerk had a stiff brightness. "No messages."

She stood by the desk, very still. It was almost as though she were under orders to behave in a certain way. To trust Richard until she had reason to distrust him. She did not know exactly what to do. She had to say what came into her head.

"May I see the registration cards for May the tenth?"

She must be out of her head! She stared at the clerk with the same astonishment as he stared at her. Her impulse was to apologize. *That just slipped out. I meant to ask for my key.* But she stood there, her hands pressed hard against the desk. *See the registration cards!*

She could not have been turned away by any power she knew.

"May I see the registration cards for May the tenth?"

"Well—I—I'll have to—"

He disappeared abruptly into the manager's office.

She waited, feeling no less a fool than she had a minute ago but sustained by a command that seemed to come from someone else.

A man of authority, fashionably thin, appeared with no smile, no kindly greeting. The clerk slipped behind him into his own place.

"I am the manager, madam. What can I do for you?"

For the third time she said the same words. "May I see the registration cards for May the tenth?"

He looked at her with a glance of absurd penetration as though he had cultivated some arcane gift. He studied her face. She kept her eyes on him. He lifted his dark brows, said something to the clerk and withdrew to his office. But she was sure that he stood just inside the door.

She held the cards in her hand and wondered, in dismay, what she was looking for. Turning them over slowly one by one she knew she was studying the handwriting on each. Richard's handwriting? Why should Richard register under a false name? The idea was so crazy that she faltered. There were not many registrations for the tenth, about a dozen. The women could be set aside. That left the names of five men. She looked at each for a long time—ages, it seemed, though in fact only long enough for a fellow guest to ask for her mail and receive it and comment on the weather.

She came back to one and examined it intently. Martin Doer, Rutland, Va. Rutland. Rutland, Va., not Vt. Was it a signal? Was it Richard's handwriting? It was! But was it? The whole thing was crazy. She was crazy, making kid melodrama. But she could not let go of the card. *Martin*. Richard made the M of Maddy just like that. . . . Sayer. Doer. The old family joke came back to her sharply. "Every sayer is a doer or he'll have to cook his words for supper."

She pushed the card to the clerk. "What room is Mr. Doer in?"

The clerk's glance flickered to the card. "He vacated his room on the eleventh."

It was Richard's handwriting. The small lobby was terribly still. A middle-aged man sat nearby reading his paper, and the rustle of turning sheets crashed on her ears. A smell of brass polish hung like a weight in the air.

She said to the clerk, "My brother signed that card."

He looked at her quickly with an expression of total opacity. His mouth opened and closed without a sound.

"Do you remember him?"

The clerk shook his head energetically. "So many people come in here, miss."

"It's his handwriting," she said stubbornly.

"How can you be so sure?" The manager was standing in the door to his office.

She hesitated for a moment and looked down at the message from Richard. It *was* a message. It had to be with all these component parts.

"Because—because there's a family joke in it and—and other signs. Please describe Mr. Doer."

The manager said, "I never saw him."

The clerk's glance wavered. When Maddy looked at him he shrugged.

She turned away badly shaken, stumbling over her shoulder bag which she had put on the floor. "Don't you remember at all—how he left?"

The clerk said nothing. The manager replied, "How he left? There could not have been anything unusual about it or we would have remembered."

The manager waited until she was on the lift. Then he said sharply to the clerk, "Destroy that card."

"Destroy—!"

"That's what I told you two days ago."

"But she's seen it now and can ask for it again."

"Have an accident. Use that bloody imagination of yours. You did it. You mend it."

Maddy shut her door and locked it. Locking was a reflex. Whenever she wanted to think at home she locked her door. If you are alone in a city which has never before felt the tread of your foot it is better to be young and indignant than knowing and experienced.

Why would Richard sign a false name?

Because he was going on an innocent vacation with his sister?

Because he did not want to be recognized?

Because he was afraid of something?

She added up what she knew, a thimbleful: he had arrived in London, for that was his signature at the bank; he had come to the hotel, for that was his handwriting on the card. Then he had disappeared.

Cloris . . . He had changed his name and disappeared with Cloris.

But that penny no longer dropped. Why would he have to change his name to go to his wife?

She sat on the edge of the bed, her face in her hands.

Go to the police. Go back to the embassy.

She made a tremendous effort at control but she had to admit that, for the first time in her life, she was alone on a large sea and did not know how to take soundings.

Find Cloris! Was that really the best thing to do or was she simply trying to hitch onto someone who knew Richard?

She picked up a thread and put it carefully in the wastebasket.

Go to the police.

Police were not sympathetic adjuncts to the life style of a nineteen-year-old American. She did not give the police serious thought.

Call home and ask advice?

Father would arrive on the next plane; where did that get them?

She was grown up. She had sense. She was Richard's confidante. He had told her he was troubled. If he was doing something secret, private and legitimate he would not want her raising a racket for the whole world to hear.

26

She sensed that some kind of truth lay in all these ambiguities and that for a time she had to trust her own
groping instincts. She tried to imagine what Richard would
want her to do.

Cloris. The name kept ringing in her head. The message
was urgent.

Why don't I want to find her?

She took a deep shuddering breath to free herself. If it's
Cloris, then it's Cloris. I'll have to face up to her.

Cloris What? Cloris Where?

She searched in her bag for her address book. But of
course Cloris was not there. Richard's wife, living in Lusaka, would not be in her address book. She had no more
idea where Cloris lived—in London or outside London—
than did that bulldog of a manager. Putting the telephone
directory with the "S's" on the floor, she went through the
"Sayers" on her hands and knees.

No Mrs. R. Sayer, or Mrs. Richard Sayer or Mrs. Cloris
Sayer, or any variation of spelling.

Perhaps Cloris was listed by her unmarried name. Then
Maddy sat back on her heels. Cloris's name before Richard
was as unremembered as yesterday's clouds.

Maddy was aghast. She must have known the name once.
She lay with her forehead pressed against the Sayers in the
telephone directory, fighting for recollection, thus driving
every clue straight out of her head.

After a long time she sat up defeated but calm. Finding
Cloris was now a prime necessity. It was all that made any
sense.

Unless appealing to his office in Lusaka for some light on
his activities made even greater sense! Say, "Richard has
vanished. Is that something you told him to do?"

If they had not told him to vanish they might take a very
dim view of the whole matter and she, Maddy, might lose
him his job.

She sat on the floor desperately trying to sort out a sudden tumbled chaos of confusion which slid over her like a collapsing tent.

Find Cloris.

At length she scrambled to her feet. She needed someone else to take a look at her thinking. This meant trusting. She trusted George and Sandra and Norman. A strange thing. Maybe their generation had figured out something about trust. You did not analyze it. You simply moved with a common understanding.

The clerk gave a start when she passed the desk but she was not even aware of him.

She went back to The Chelsea Pantry. The Frenchwoman at the cash register was working on accounts. She said "Hallo" and "How foolish" as she compared receipts and finally, "We don't serve dinner till six."

"I am trying to find some people I had dinner with yesterday. I think they come often. I don't know their last names. Their first names were George and Sandra and Norman."

The woman gave this deep thought, tapping her cheek with her pencil as she stared out of the window.

"There are many names like that in here."

"Norman had a long red mustache. George had a beard."

The woman laughed. "Dozens!"

"I think George makes jewelry."

"So—maybe George Carmichael. The wife is small and ugly?"

"Ugly?"

"*Belle laide*. Sandra, yes, that's her name. And the red mustache—yes, they're always together. The red mustache goes to the Polytechnical College. Sandra weaves and George makes jewelry. They have a shop. Now I will think for a moment. . . . Turn left down the King's Road. Go to the Polytechnical College. The shop is a few steps one way or the other."

The young man who had ridden from the airport with Maddy came into the hotel and went to the door of the manager's office. His knock was perfunctory.

The manager did not greet him, contenting himself with a baleful look. The young man leaned on the desk.

"Oliver said if I were passing to find out what questions she's been asking."

" 'She'?"

"You know very well."

"Oliver can jolly well do his own jobs after this! It's intolerable." The elegant manager tugged painfully at the tufts of hair which grew on his cheekbones. "She recognized the handwriting on a registration card. I thought the card had been destroyed. I don't want any part of this!"

"Oh, come now . . ." The young man sat down slowly.

King's Road was as crowded as yesterday. Maddy had not realized she was tense until she relaxed. This kind of crowd was no crowd; it was home. She paused outside a window of Swedish clothes and saw a blouse for her mother.

Then she remembered she did not have enough money to buy blouses for anyone until she caught up with Richard, so she began looking for the Polytechnic College.

She saw Sandra through the shop window, and Sandra saw her at the same time. Sandra's face broke into a smile, showing her big teeth in her small face. She beckoned eagerly.

"How's your brother?" she asked in her thin little voice.

"He hasn't shown up. That's why I wanted to talk with you."

George had sold a ring to a youth who went out admiring it on his finger, and now George leaned both elbows on the counter and said, "What's up?" as though Richard were shared.

"He was here—he was in London—he was at the hotel. Now he's disappeared."

"Norman's good at things like this," George said to Sandra. "Phone him and find out what he thinks."

"His classes are breaking. In actual fact, he'll be here directly."

Maddy leaned against the wall. "I must find his wife. They're separated. But there's no Cloris Sayer in the telephone book and I don't know her unmarried name."

"Never?"

"I suppose I did once."

"Then you'll have to remember it again, won't you? Concentrate." Sandra put her face close to Maddy's. "*Think*."

"I have. Everything flies."

"Relax."

"I've tried. I thought maybe he'd gone to her and gotten so involved he'd like me to go home. Then something else happened and I'm not so sure. But I keep getting her name. Doesn't that mean something—when you keep getting a name?"

"Oh, yes."

Maddy said, rather shyly and apologetically, "I had to talk to you."

"Of course."

When Norman came, he was casual and laconic but patted Maddy's head with a grin. Sandra said, "You must think very well, Norman. Maddy has not heard anything from her brother. What shall we do?"

Norman leaned on the counter and studied Maddy.

"Begin at the beginning."

She told of the bank, the embassy and the hotel card.

"You're sure it was his writing on the hotel card?"

"Yes."

"Dead sure? You'd go to prison for it?"

"I'm sure!"

"Because sometimes you want to believe something very much. Isn't that so?"

30

"The 'M' and the family joke, and Rutland—"

"I just want you to be sure."

She was silent. Of course she was sure . . . but she wished she could see the card again.

"You're convinced he got safely to London? We don't need to start at the airport?"

"I'm sure."

Norman, still leaning against the counter, chewed his mustache and studied the floor with a frown.

"Pot? Acid?"

"No."

"A bird?"

She did not understand. "A girl friend?"

"Maybe he's gone back to his wife."

George was putting away trays of jewelry and turning off lights. "Then it's his business."

"Yes, but I have to know."

George said, "For ten bob we can get a good dinner at The Bamboo Drum. Shall we go?"

"Most people have a whimsy of some kind, don't they?" Norman asked, his hands in his pockets, his head bent low, as they waited for George to lock the shop door. "Give it a thought. Africa . . . what kind of whimsy?"

"It's as though a door opened and he was pushed down a chute," George said cheerfully, looking in his shop window to smooth down his hair and beard.

"Why do people disappear?" Sandra asked, folding the two curtains of her long hair behind her ears. "They do it all the time. Quite normal."

Quite normal. Maddy frowned. Yes . . . but *Martin Doer* meant something else.

The Bamboo Drum was Chinese and quiet. Sandra drew her bare feet under her on the leatherette seat and repeated her question. "Why *do* people disappear? We've got a problem and we must look at it all round."

"They want a holiday," George said. "They can't pay their bills. They've stopped loving their bird. Or love a new one. Or—just go."

"What would you do if your brother didn't show up? In New York."

"In New York! Leave him to God."

"If my brother disappeared," Norman said, gravely studying his chopsticks, "I'd do nothing. It's his life."

"If he were sick!"

Norman turned his green eyes and looked intently at Maddy. "He'd get well." Then he saw her expression and smiled faintly. "Or he'd telephone."

"If George were lost," Sandra said, "I'd know why and I'd do something."

"What?" George asked with interest.

"It would depend on why you got lost." She was wispy but indomitable.

"In a strange city!" Maddy urged.

Sandra thought intently, her small narrow face without expression.

"I'd go to the police."

The staggering simplicity of this convention opened Maddy's eyes very wide. "You have to be joking!"

"Or put a word in the personals." George stirred his tea. " 'Brother please send word Maddy grieving.' "

"That's what I'd do," Sandra said. "The police. Unless I thought I knew where George was. Shall we go to the police?" She brushed the strands of hair from her face as she looked at Maddy. Her smile was very gentle.

"What can I tell them?"

"The police get the B.B.C. to ask about missing people every night." Norman put his egg roll on her empty plate.

"What do I know?" She ate the egg roll absently.

"What you've told us. You don't need to go alone. We'll go with you."

She was as taut as a sling. *Why can't I go to the police? Why can't I? What's the matter with me?* She felt an odd desolation. A faith in tribal wisdom had not been justified. She was back with her own intuition, misty, incoherent, but adamant.

"He hoped I would do just what I did—and read his message. Then what did he expect me to do?"

"He called himself Doer—he's doing it."

She looked quickly at George. "I've got to know."

"Why? It's his life."

"I'm beginning to feel helpless. I hate that."

"I'd want to know too," Sandra said, as inassertive as a parachute carrying its full load to earth.

George looked at her with a mild alarm.

"Police? Let's go," Norman said.

Very quietly Maddy said "No," and then almost as quietly she said, "Payne—that's her name."

"Oh! Cloris?" Sandra took her hand briefly. "Where's the telephone?"

Maddy was already on her feet. "If she's not listed, I'll call all the Paynes. One might be her parents."

But with Sandra's chin on her shoulder, their forefingers working in tandem, Payne, Cloris, was the third listing.

"My throat feels like flannel." Maddy fumbled for a coin. "I can't swallow." The double ring went on for a moment, then a woman's voice said "Hullo," brisk and high.

"Cloris Payne? Are you Cloris Payne Sayer? Oh, Cloris, this is Madeline, Richard's sister. Yes, I'm in London. Is Richard with you? Oh . . . Have you seen him? Cloris, he sent me a cable where to meet him—yesterday—but he hasn't come."

Cloris's voice was very clear. Sandra could hear her as well as Maddy. "We're divorcing, you know."

"Yes, I know—but may I talk with you—Oh, thank you. Right away. Give me the address."

At the table, George said, "That's not far—South Ken."

On the street Norman put his arm across Maddy's shoulders. "Okay?"

"Yes."

"You're a good bird. You care. Lovely."

Her heart swelled with gratitude but one did not use many words.

George called back, "That hotel—do you think they are putting you on?"

"I don't know."

George's voice rose above traffic. "Did they think you would go to the police?"

"I didn't say I would. Should I?"

"Don't leave! Stick there. Ask questions!"

She looked at Norman. "Questions?"

He licked his red mustache. "The chambermaid, for example—ask if she can remember this Martin Doer. That kind of thing."

In a group they found 30 Drayton Gardens and stood looking at it. Norman succinctly appraised its economic status in the scheme of values. George wrote down his shop's telephone number. "But come around tomorrow. Let us know. Saturday is a big bash but come."

"Five bob it's the first floor," Norman said. "There's a blonde. You see her and then you don't." He gave Maddy a little push. "Jump in."

As she searched for the bell to Cloris's flat she knew they stood together in the road, waiting. When the door clicked she waved and they turned slowly down the road.

"Madeline?" said Cloris at the top of the stairs. "What a nasty business for you. Too bad of Richard, I must say. Well, how do you do? I never thought I'd meet you in this way. Richard was forever planning for you to come to Lusaka. In you go. We're just having coffee. This is Aidan Ross. It never occurred to me we wouldn't meet in Lusaka.

You know Richard's job had him always on the move. Perhaps he's just got stuck—no phone, no telegraph, broken-down Land Rover with no black boy to fix it."

Eddies of poise and scent and fashionableness flowed toward Maddy. She had the impression of a yellow and white room, very chic, with a white and golden Cloris in the center. For a moment she was out of her depth, unpoised, uncertain, unsophisticated, but she struggled to recover her footing.

"He was in London on the tenth," she said, looking from one to the other.

"But I thought you said—!"

"Do sit down," Aidan Ross said. "I knew Richard a bit."

At this she turned toward him as though he had switched on a light.

"Please sit down." He drew out a white Italian chair. "Since you called we've been puzzling."

"Don't ask her any questions till I've got the coffee."

Maddy did not take her eyes from this man who knew Richard a bit. Tangible and human. Taller than Richard, she thought, perhaps a bit older, more slender, more contained. "Contained." What in the world did she mean by that? Resources? Confidence?

In any event she kept looking at him. Go on—talk! her eyes said. He offered her a cigarette, which she refused, still waiting for some direction. He sat near her, on the arm of the sofa, a dark figure, dark suit, dark hair, dark very clear eyes. They seemed unsurprised, his eyes, not at all judgmental.

Then she turned away, frowning a little and glancing around the room. She was always doing that, she told herself impatiently—getting deep thoughts about people's eyes.

"You know Richard." She made it a statement rather than a question.

He nodded. "Where did you come from yesterday?"

35

"Boston." Her glance slipped around the room again. "How do you know Richard?" Though Richard was her primary concern this room also made a demand. Richard's wife's flat. It perplexed her for reasons she did not understand. She looked about the beautiful room quickly and furtively, the plaster work on the high ceiling, the long windows curtained in white and gold, the opulent furniture so cunningly mixed: the Regency sofa, where Aidan sat watching her, living harmoniously with the white Italian chairs cushioned in lemon and tangerine.

He had not answered. He smiled at her when she looked at him again.

"It's a beautiful room, isn't it?" he said.

She nodded. "How do you know Richard?"

"I met him soon after he came to Zambia. I'm a Rhodesian."

She struggled with a dozen questions and fashioned one "I never really understood his job. What was it?"

"He was responsible for a kind of resources study, developing water potentials. Statistical. Interesting."

"Very dull!" Cloris said crisply as she put down the coffee tray with a jingle of bracelets and a nervous grace "But full of tricks. His job. You know that, Aidan—all those jobs have a touch of diplomacy. Suddenly everything becomes very finger-to-lips."

"Dangerous?" Maddy asked.

"Not at all. Just closed-mouth and chancy. Or so 'it seemed to me. Black or white? The coffee!"

"Oh—black."

"Now!" Cloris sat on a tangerine cushion and looked at Maddy over the rim of her cup. "Miserable Richard. Tell us all."

Maddy found that she was rubbing one sandaled foot gently back and forth on the thick gold rug and wondering how Richard's wife paid for all this. It must cost a million dollars unless the flat belonged to someone else. Yet it fitted Cloris, as any fool could see. Cloris's fine pale hair, worn high with fashionable ringlets against her cheeks, had great affinity with the subtle color of the walls, as though a good deal of thought had been given to both. Her eyes were small but the careful make-up heightened their brilliance. Her dress was simple to the point of ostentation but her legs were so spectacular that Maddy drew her own beautiful legs out of sight and competition.

Suddenly she did not wish to tell all or anything. Not for the moment anyway. The precise immediate demand on her thoughts was Cloris. Cloris was supposed to lead her to Richard—that's all. Not raise other questions. But Maddy was intensely aware of this thin and elegant, quick and nervous woman who seemed totally unrelated to the Richard she knew.

She felt most subtly dislocated as though a perfectly clear focus had been tampered with or as though her equilibrium had been altered by a hair's breadth. A wild, disarraying thought fogged her mind for a moment; perhaps Richard hated Cloris and would be aghast if Maddy poured out the mystery of his disappearance.

It was terribly disturbing. She almost stood up to go, collecting a jumble of explanations. A candid realism intervened; Cloris would make mincemeat of any improvised excuse. And Aidan Ross would continue to look remarkably deep and quizzical and attractive, demanding to be trusted. Moreover she was here because some persistent intuition had thrust Cloris into her thoughts again and again.

She made herself relax and lean back but she was still cautious, her account cut to the bone—of Richard's signature at the bank and of his failure to register at the embassy. With great resolution she blotted from her mind all temptation to tell Cloris of the distress signal run up by "Martin Doer."

"So." Cloris's eyes were wide and her brows lifted. She looked at Aidan. "He reached London. Aidan, what do you make of all this?"

"Was Richard always very punctual?"

"Absurdly. An appointment was a meeting with God. I did say to Maddy that his job had him all over the place, but he always telephoned or sent a wire if he were delayed."

"This second cable about a will—was he the kind of man who took out flight insurance for an hour in the air?"

"No," Cloris answered, twisting a ringlet.

He looked at Maddy. "I think the bank could be obliged to open that deedbox."

"I want Richard, not the deedbox." Keeping Richard alive in her thoughts was the best way she knew to control panic.

After a moment, his eyes on her, he murmured, "Fair enough."

"Does his company have an office in London?"

"No," Cloris said sharply. "Everything was based in the United States."

"Might he have gotten in touch with some of his friends, or yours, in London?"

"I don't know any of his friends here. We met in Lusaka when I was staying with my sister. We spent our honeymoon in France. If he knew people in London he never mentioned them. Really, it's most mystifying." She shook down her bracelets, playing the melody of silver against gold. A frown was pinched between her eyes. "Say something more, Aidan."

"I'm lost in thought." He studied Cloris briefly. His smile had faded. "There's one man in London he might have seen —but that man asked me today when Richard was coming." He glanced at Maddy. "We could cable the office in Lusaka—see if he had been given any special assignment for the two days before he met you."

"How would you put it so they wouldn't go into a spin if he had no assignment?"

"Or had assigned himself a girl friend for two days," Cloris added without rancor.

Aidan did not reply. He leaned forward, his hands clasped in front of his mouth.

"A friend might undertake it—Neil Allingham, Cloris."

"Neil has been transferred to Lagos." She looked at Maddy. "I shouldn't worry. He was a bit rocked when I left him. That's nearly four months ago, I agree, but he has very little time to himself in Lusaka. I suspect it all came over him in a rush and he's hiding his heart someplace."

In Maddy anger shot into a flame. "Why did you leave him?"

Cloris was astonished. A faint flush colored her face. She answered sharply. "You can't go on loving a filing cabinet and a Dictaphone forever."

"That's not Richard."

"You aren't Richard's wife. He was the coldest man I ever knew. My ambitions aren't built on a glacier."

Richard a glacier? Richard *the coldest man I ever knew*? Something in Maddy drew back and closed up. Cloris touched Maddy's leg with the toe of her elegant shoe. "Sorry. Sister and wife never see a man in quite the same way. But I'd hate to have anything happen to the old fellow. It hasn't. I'm sure. He's terribly competent. If he doesn't show up in a day or so, then we should worry. Now I'd enjoy myself. Wouldn't you agree, Aidan? Would you like to go shopping with me tomorrow?"

Maddy whispered, "I'd like to find Richard tomorrow."

Cloris sat up very straight, the lovely mound of breast somewhat unreal. "He *is* a beast. I'm cross with him for treating you like this. It's too naughty. What do you want me to do?"

"Remember anything that might help."

She did not like Cloris. Suddenly she did not trust Cloris, or anyone or anything in this room. She felt responsibility closing over her like a tide and she had not the slightest wisdom or guide for the future. She felt a fool, a kid, sitting there in her short hair, turtle-neck sweater, corduroy jumper, heelless shoes, and looking at them out of big brown eyes!

She frowned. She *was* a kid and she *did* have on a jumper and she *didn't* know what to do. She'd have to make the best of it by using her common sense. She stood up.

"Don't go," Cloris said.

"He told me to be at the hotel. I don't like to stay away too long."

"You look such a baby," Cloris said, "with that cropped hair. People probably push you about. Do they?"

Maddy looked at her for a moment. "No."

"I'll ring for a taxi. How are you for money?" Not waiting for a reply to her question, Cloris dialed a number. When she turned away from her phone, she opened her purse. "Here's five pounds. No, no, take it. I'll ring you tomorrow—or you ring me, whichever you like. Be sure to talk with me."

Maddy tried again. "Cloris, you must know something. You don't mean you can't help!"

"What are you saying?"

"It's *Richard.* You must know something. You must have a suggestion!"

Cloris became very silent. Noiselessly she smoothed her bracelets against her arm. She looked at Maddy coldly. "Why should I? He's out of my life."

They heard the taxi arrive. Maddy put the five pounds under a book as Cloris went into the hall to call down to the driver. Aidan touched her hand. "I'll put you in the taxi," he said, but Cloris came along too, with a return of charm.

"You've got a look about you like Richard," she said. "It makes me rather miss the old goose." She kissed Maddy.

40

"Now remember—I am still your sister-in-law. Ring me tomorrow."

Aidan said nothing. Maddy ducked into the taxi, muttering goodbye. Aidan paid the taxi driver and then his face appeared for a moment at the window and he raised his hand. Looking out of the back window, she saw him take Cloris's arm and lead her back toward the house.

Passing through the dark streets she felt as though moving through a great void. "I won't go back home without hearing Richard's voice," she said aloud.

This steadied her, for now she was convinced that Richard was in terrible danger—convinced, prickly with alarm, unable to appraise it, very lonely. With a sort of sheltering anger (for the sudden fear was too much to bear naked) she asked why Richard had married Cloris. Where did he fit into a world so elegant, nervous, expensive and implausible?

And who was this Aidan Ross? She turned on him, for he too was a part of the sudden, unfamiliar dread. In love with Cloris? Undermining Richard with those warm dark eyes? As attractive as her brother but not her brother?

She had desperately sought Cloris and had found her and received a plateful of mischief and confusion.

The coldest man I've ever known. . . . This more than anything else had appalled her. This was not the Richard who wrote about walking in Scotland. *My ambitions are not built on a glacier.* But that apartment was not furnished with pennies!

She was suddenly desperately tired. Still keyed to expect a message, she glanced toward the desk and saw something in her mailbox.

Because of a previous booking your room will be required at noon tomorrow. Respectfully, The Management. Exhaustion was overlaid by stubborn anger. She looked at the clerk.

"I will not be leaving. Please tell the manager."

She ran for the lift before he could answer. She locked and bolted her door. She even put a chair against it and sat on the chair, saying aloud, "I will not leave until I find out what happened to Martin Doer."

Reaction she said to herself sturdily when she began to shiver. Putting on her coat did not help. She walked back and forth, fighting against certain facts which she had not wished to consider. After a time she stopped fighting. They could not be evaded. Use your common sense.

Sharp as a knife was the fact that she was totally ignorant of Richard's life. She loved him but she did not know a thing about his life.

She repeated it aloud on the principle that honesty would force open a door. "I love him but I don't know a thing about his life."

She stared at this fact. She forced herself to face it. In his letter he had written, "I can't even see myself any more or hear my own voice." She did not know whether his job was good or bad. She did not know whether he had bartered his soul, or whether he had disappeared because he had to go or because he was sick or because he had been kidnapped or because he was dead.

Maybe searching for him was putting him in terrible danger.

Now she was really afraid.

Aidan Ross unlocked the door of the flat and, before he took off his raincoat, went to the telephone.

The operator told him a call to Rhodesia might take some time to get through. He made tea while he waited and walked about sipping it, trying to control his black impatience. He turned on the television and turned it off because the fool's face made the darker realities intolerably poignant. He took up the evening paper and, standing, read the leader, but the strike negotiations in Newcastle were such an exercise in abstractions that he resisted all understanding.

The telephone rang and he seized it.

"Miles? Are you able to talk? You must tell me something. You're the only person I trust. I had a call from Alfie."

"Alfie?"

"My joke. I thought you understood. Alfie's my Internal Security keeper. He said that Richard had stolen a file of the utmost importance. I think he's lying."

"Why?" The faraway voice was cool and a little sleepy.

"Richard doesn't steal!"

"How can you be so sure?"

Aidan said angrily, "Because I am. What do you know?"

Miles hesitated. "That snippet was fed into the computer of high-level gossip. To see the reaction? To cover up something else? I don't know. After all, Richard's expendable. He's American."

"Then you don't believe it either?"

"It sounds a bit stupid, not like Richard."

"He's missing."

"What!"

"Have you any ideas?"

"Look, old chap, if Richard has made any false step the Americans will have to fish him out. It's all my life's worth to know a thing. I've got a full plate. Shall I tell you the latest? Mutti has been arrested."

"My God! Have you seen him?"

"Seen him? Are you mad? He's incommunicado."

"It's true? No question about it?"

"Well, what is truth, dear chump? I've every reason to think it's a fact, however."

"Can you make it fit in with Richard in any way?"

After a long silence Miles said lightly, "I can try."

43

"If Mutti is harmed, the repercussions will not stop with Rhodesia."

"Oh, very nearly I agree." Then brightly, as though waking up. "Have they put the screws on you?"

Aidan said violently, "I was a fool to come. It's a monstrous position. I'm like a tethered goat."

"See nothing, hear nothing, say nothing, get the export-import signature and come home. You'll be all right."

"No thanks for poor advice."

Miles said more gravely, "Keep in touch but ever so cunningly."

To Maddy her room was a prison. Opening the window, she leaned into the darkness. The street was quiet. The King's Road traffic murmured in the distance. If she was putting Richard in danger she had to be told. If she was his only friend at the moment she had to be wise. All she knew for certain was that he was her brother. And that she had to act with blind faith in the brother she knew.

Did she dare leave out the police or the embassy any longer? Why was the hotel trying to make her leave?

"I'm very stubborn," she said aloud. "And I know that mysteries exist for the sole purpose of being solved."

But as she stumbled to bed all her inexperience and inadequacy folded around her suffocatingly. Her first job was to refuse to be suffocated.

She sat up in bed, in the half-dark. When she fell asleep she was sitting up against the pillows.

The Third Day

In the morning she began to dress the moment she wakened. Lying in bed invited waves of confusion. People hated helpless people. So did she.

When the maid brought her breakfast Norman's voice came back to her. *Speak to the chambermaid.*

But a trolley of breakfast trays proved insurmountable.

Could the management make her leave? If she allowed them to put her out of the hotel she would break the only tenuous link she had with "Martin Doer." She crumbled her roll and absently fed herself with small pieces.

Within any reasonable term of reference, some action had to be taken. Yet something still and strong kept re-iterating, *Wait. This hotel holds a clue.*

"What am I supposed to do?" she asked aloud, walking back and forth. "Take this place apart room by room? Oh, come on, God, that's crazy." To the window, to the door, back and forth; by her presence refusing to yield the room yet conscious of the fact that she must not trap herself within these square feet.

When the telephone rang, she sprang to answer it. Richard—the management—Norman?

"Madeline? This is Aidan Ross. Hello! Are you there?"

She laughed faintly. "Yes."

"Will you lunch with me?"

She remembered the way he had put his hand on Cloris's arm as Maddy drove away in the taxi. "Why?"

"Because I want to talk with you."

"What about?"

"Madeline, I told you I am Richard's friend."

She was silent.

"Oh, for God's sake—" His voice sounded tired. "It's not as important to me as it might be to Richard." His dark eyes, dark voice became very vivid.

"I'm sorry."

"There's an Italian restaurant on King's Road at Church Street. A ten-minute walk for you. One o'clock?" He sounded very remote.

"I'll be there."

She was stiff with inexperience and caution. She would look at Aidan coolly. She would ask questions and seize any scrap of a hint. If Richard were alive and well then everything was right on. If Richard were alive and in danger then he might be saved by some clue from the heady darkness of Aidan Ross.

When a knock came at the door she was ready for anything and threw open the door with a defiance that unnerved the tall young maid whose arms were full of bed linen and a carpet sweeper.

Speak to the chambermaid.

The maid was surprised and apologetic. She had been told the room was vacant.

"I'm not leaving," Maddy said. "Come in. You can make the bed now. I'd like to talk to you if you don't mind."

The maid was wary. She came into the room with her pale eyes fixed on Maddy. She put down the carpet sweeper and linen, her glance still guarded, though a small light of curiosity began to break when Maddy leaned against the door and said, "I need your help."

"Oh?" Her hands took care of the bedmaking as she watched Maddy over her shoulder.

"My brother sent me a cable to meet him here last Thursday. But he wasn't here. And the manager said he has never been here. But I think he has. Will you please help me by remembering? Please! Has an American been in the hotel in the last four days? He's twenty-seven years old, sandy-haired, medium height. He dresses well, he's a businessman—"

The girl turned away, presenting a round neat rump and long thick legs. She did not answer until she gave a last smooth to the bed. "We get a fair number of Americans, tourists, I should say. I mind this floor, miss. There was no such gentleman here. But on the third floor—well, the girl that minds that said a gentleman was after taking his sister to Scotland, right to the top, Tongue, and there's where I live and I got tears in my eyes. Though why is a wonder, for I'd never go back unless it was for a million pounds."

The blood rushed to Maddy's head. "Where can I find this girl?"

"Well now, it's her day off today."

"Where does she live?"

"Lambeth."

"Where is Lambeth? Oh—have you ever been completely alone in a strange place, thinking your brother may be hurt, not knowing what to do?"

"Well, I can't say that I have, can I? Lambeth's across the river. You take number ten bus at Victoria—now where does she live? I'll just go ask."

"Don't say why you're asking."

"No—why not? Wouldn't Housekeeper be a one to ask?"

Maddy hesitated. "She's the management. There's something I don't quite understand about the management."

With wonderful good sense the girl laughed.

While she was gone, Maddy put on her suit, brushed her hair, found her shoes, looked at the time, considered her meager funds carefully. No dreams of a taxi to Lambeth.

The girl slipped back into the room like a conspirator. "There you are. It's twenty-five Maria Street. She's Maureen O'Connell. You get off number ten at St. George's Road. Two streets over."

Maddy gave her a quick embrace. "Will you try to remember anything else?"

"Aye, that I will."

The manager was at the desk. She went up to him coolly. "I am staying here until I find my brother."

He smiled—which produced a terrifying effect. "Your room has been booked for someone else."

She smiled as falsely as he.

"You can't put me out. If you try I will get a policeman." Her voice was small but it carried.

When such a commanding man looks indignant, the indignation is awful. Lightning flashes in the eyes. The clerk stole a look. Maddy held onto the desk.

"I've got proof he was in this hotel. If you'd just help me I would get out of here today."

"Proof!" Contempt, derision, and, she thought, fear invested the word, all wrung through his public and impersonal manner. "Take care what you say, young lady. This is a respectable hotel and we are protected by the law."

"So am I," she said and went out to the street.

Something was beginning to break. Richard was a little nearer.

King's Road was jammed with the Saturday crowd. Outside the pubs, patrons stood on the sidewalk in the sunlight, drinks in their hands, within a cacophony of talk. On the road itself traffic crawled to the shriek of horns, and when she reached Old Church Street, she saw that the

48

traffic had to be breasted to reach the restaurant. But it all piled up courteously to wave her across and when she gained the other side she paused in the sunlight to reflect on the pell-mell good nature which seemed so familiar and yet so different.

The restaurant was small, energetic and crowded. It took her a moment to separate the people with her eyes and find Aidan, rising from a table near the window. He was smiling as a waiter drew out her chair, and he continued to smile as they sat opposite each other in mutual survey.

"I'm glad you've come."

She was not sure what she felt, so her smile was more fleeting.

He was even more attractive than she remembered. But she was tough with herself. She knew she always got involved at a moment's notice because she liked people. This, however, was something more subtle. She tried to see him as an unknown quantity, assets and liabilities undefined, related to her crisis only through the ambiguous element called Cloris.

But because she was so unfamiliar with caution she knew she might be overreacting; she might be sifting everything through such a fine mesh that in the end she would learn nothing at all.

"What will you have for lunch? They've very good—"

"Salad and a glass of milk."

"Are you quite sure?" He looked a little dismayed.

"Yes."

"A glass of wine?"

"No."

He murmured, "Richard's sister!" as he studied the menu.

When he had given his order she said, "Why did you say, 'Richard's sister'?"

"Oh—" He was briefly amused. "A salad, yes—he might order that—but never a glass of milk. Well, never mind.

49

Now, are we to enjoy ourselves first or come straight to business?"

If she was to be at a disadvantage, she was determined it was not to be on the basis of a nineteen-year-old, milk-drinking American.

"I want to know why I'm here."

He studied her for a moment. "Business first. Very well." He stared out of the window for a moment in silence. When he looked at her his dark eyes were grave.

"When you appeared at Cloris's flat, searching for Richard, I was shaken. I too was expecting to meet him this week and I too had received no message."

If he wished to have her entire attention he had succeeded.

"Oh. . . . Why didn't you say so last night?"

"Caution, when I realized that Cloris is no friend of Richard. I tried to go alone with you to the taxi but I failed."

"Where were you meeting him? When?"

"Right here, as a matter of fact. Last Wednesday at lunch. I waited till three o'clock. And I came back the next day."

"Why were you meeting him?"

He hesitated and the dark, rather sad, face clouded. "Never mind. Perhaps I'll tell you another time."

A confusion of relief and helplessness swept over her. As though some amorphous evil was about to be substantiated and dealt with, or, at the other extreme, a very simple explanation adduced. She leaned back in her chair; nothing existed at the moment but Aidan and what he might have to say. She felt older than time and a biologic extension of Richard.

Aidan, watching intently, said, "You've no doubt that he intended to go to Scotland with you?"

"No."

He gave a peculiar little sigh. "Nor I." He hesitated, his

50

long fingers crumbling a piece of bread. He looked at her suddenly as though making up his mind. "I know Richard very well. I'm not just a casual friend. We've trusted each other in many ways. Cloris never knew this. Do you have a political mind?"

"Instincts."

"An interest in African politics?"

"If it involves Richard."

He said gently, "Eat your salad."

"I am." But she wasn't.

"Will you have an ice?" She shook her head. "Coffee?"

"Yes, please."

He gave the order and indicated that he would not finish his lunch. Leaning on the table he looked at her with a frown.

"I told you I'm a Rhodesian. I came to London a fortnight ago on business. Zambia was Northern Rhodesia until 1964. But that doesn't separate one, not for a long time—a generation perhaps." He was formal and courteous, trying her out. "Zambia has a black government. We've got a lily-white one, blacks in detention camps, apartheid threatened. Zambia and Rhodesia behave very correctly, but other things go on as well. Rhodesians are tense. We walk on eggs." He looked at her and smiled rather diffidently. "I'm not a believer in the lily-white, nor is Richard. But I'm not a revolutionist though I think perhaps Richard is. I did what I could while Rhodesia was still in the Commonwealth. After that . . . I wait and hope we'll come to our senses. Richard thought I was too prudent. I thought he needed curbing. A foreign-aid expert, a guest in a black African country—where relations are very sticky with white Africa to the south—needs some complicated restraints. He has to talk without acting much of the time. I am not sure how carefully Richard proportioned the two. He knew black Rhodesians who had escaped the dragnet and got to

51

Zambia. He was also in Rhodesia every month or so." He shrugged slightly. "If he messed about he was idiotic whatever his intentions. I think he did a bit." She watched him intently and now was acutely aware of his eyes, very alive, examining her closely. "Yet what could he do?"

She frowned. "Are you asking me?"

"If you care to reply."

"I don't even know what you mean."

"If he carried messages and got caught, Rhodesians might hold him overnight in a jail until some consul came on the run; then he would become *persona non grata* and we would see him back to Zambia where he would become a liability and presently be returned to Boston. Isn't that what would happen?"

" 'We.' 'We' might arrest him. . . ."

"Not me. Do be sensible! Even if he carried a message to England—there are black Rhodesians here; I have a message or two to deliver—it would be part of a game and never serious enough to cause a man like Richard to disappear from sight. May I see his letter to you?"

She started to dig in her shoulder bag and then she hesitated. The letters were very private. She was bound so inextricably to Richard that she was not yet ready to be objective. With the unexplored, unexamined, she moved with great uncertainty. She said she had left the letters at the hotel but here were his cables. She handed them to Aidan and watched him with lowered eyes. In the labyrinth of suspicions she had no guide, only her inexperience which, she sensibly knew, could deceive her again and again. Unless she refused to be deceived. . . .

Aidan read the two cables as the waiter poured coffee. He handed them back without comment. After a moment he asked, "Are you really suspicious of the hotel?"

"Yes." She glanced at him. "He *was* there."

His eyebrows shot up. "Ah?"

"An American who talked of taking his sister to Scotland was in the hotel this week."

"Who told you?"

"I heard it . . . by accident." Her caution startled her. Or inexperience? She was restless with both.

"I'll go and talk to them!"

"No! Please."

"Don't you trust me?" He spoke without stress.

She flushed and tried to answer.

Aidan said, "I suppose you've got only my word for who I am. I *am* Richard's friend." He smiled slightly, not looking at her. "I'll have to find a way to prove it." Then he said in his slow deep voice, "Of course *I* don't know that you're his sister. You could have sent those cables to yourself. Shall we find a way to trust each other?"

She wanted to believe all things, trust all things, find Richard. She said suddenly, "I don't like Cloris."

He frowned. "What's that got to do with us?"

"Why were you there?"

He stared at her. "She is the wife of my friend. I saw her for the first time in five months at a dinner last week. She said she wanted to talk with me." Exasperated, he pushed away from the table. "How absurd!"

To her fury, tears sprang to her eyes. "She said Richard was a filing cabinet and a glacier. That apartment of hers is very expensive. Does she have money?"

He answered sharply, "I've never asked anything about Cloris. I'm indifferent to her kind of woman. Richard married her, not I. Does that answer your questions?"

She put down her napkin. "I have to go."

"Where?"

She smiled faintly. "Richard's my brother, not you. . . ."

"Blast and sorry."

They went out of the restaurant not speaking, both flushed, and stood at the curb as though neither was certain of the next move. Then compulsively he touched her hair. "*You're* his sister. You're just as irritating as he is."

She grinned and ducked her head.

"Do you want a taxi?" he asked.

"No."

"May I call you tomorrow?"

She said faintly, after a pause, "I must look pretty stubborn to you. But I don't understand things." She looked at him wistfully. "I have to do what I think is right, don't I? I'll call you. Don't be angry."

"I'm not angry. I just wonder how I can make you believe me. If Richard is in trouble he needs more help than you can give him. I know you're holding something back. I can't force you to go to the police but I can go."

"And terribly mess up things for Richard. . . ."

He frowned and stared at his shoes. Neither seemed able to leave. Then he took out a diary, wrote on a sheet and handed it to her. "Here are two numbers. This one before nine and after six. Please ring me."

She took the numbers eagerly. "Thank you. I really do thank you."

"Are you sure I can't take you someplace?"

She shook her head. He held her hand for a moment. "Take care."

She nodded and walked away without saying goodbye.

My God, who is he? Trust or not trust? All her measurements were based on such simple units that she walked now in the middle of a crowd metaphorically wringing her hands. A month ago she would have treated her roommate to a package of nonsense about falling in love and they would have kidded around with nothing questioned, nothing damaged.

Fall in love but not now, when something awful was approaching. She heard it coming. Even though she did not know what it was she could not afford to be taken by surprise.

54

She did not know whether to trust or distrust the unsurprised quality in his expression. She thought that maybe he had *never* been naïve, not even as a boy. Maybe his natural gift was the one he showed her, that is, to be quiet and find out, sympathetic but not sentimental. Maybe he was the kind who would fight hard for things until he had run out of strength and then adjust himself, always trying to hold onto his options.

Maybe he was not a talker but a watcher—yet he was by no means inarticulate. She tried to fiddle with the lens so that she could focus more clearly because she needed all her common sense, faith and loyalty.

Going up King's Road in the intermittent sunlight, jostled by the crowds, hesitating at windows to untangle her commotion, she recognized that she had to master something hard and concrete in this slippery and unfamiliar world. Then she thought of Sandra, George and Norman. Their drum signals were understood, they were home and comfort and trust.

Again Sandra saw her through the window and again her thin little face broke into a wide smile as they met in the doorway.

"What happened? What is she like? Did she help?"

"Cloris?" That seemed long ago. "Help? Not really. I didn't like her. I'm back where I started. Well, not quite. I had a strange kind of lunch with a man who was with her."

"Strange?" They were talking in sibilants, half whispering, because George was selling a spectacular hammered-gold necklace to a splendid young woman in a heather-mixed suit. "Come into the back. Norman's there. Why strange?"

Norman scarcely looked up. He gave a minuscule nod and continued to write prices in beautiful calligraphy on tiny bits of stiff paper. Now, Norman she could trust without question.

Suddenly Maddy did not want to examine Aidan's strangeness. Without any real footing where he was concerned, even her common sense in danger, she had no point of judgment. "I don't know," she said. "It began to groove and then it didn't. Suddenly everything's like a crazy house. You're fat when you're thin and long when you're short."

Sandra sat on the floor against the wall, hugging her knees.

"Talk about it."

Norman looked at her briefly and gave a ghost of a grin. It was as good as a handclasp before he went back to his painstaking task, his long hair and long mustache giving a pentecostal blessing to all this commercial activity.

"Something else happened that maybe's more important." And she told about Maureen O'Connell. Norman stopped his work. Sandra struck the floor with her hand. George, forty pounds richer, listened briefly in the doorway and whistled.

"What are you waiting for?" George said. "Norman's got his car round the corner."

"It's something real, isn't it?" Maddy said. "Will you go with me, Norman?"

"Coo!" said Norman and went to wash his hands.

When Aidan reached the office near Westminster which had been put at his disposal, he found a telephone message underlined by an urgent red pencil. The secretary, hearing him, came in to reaffirm the red pencil. "His secretary promised I'd be sacked if I didn't make you salute the telephone directly you came in."

"Aren't Permanent Under Secretaries out for lunch at this hour?"

"Not this one, I should fancy."

"What's it about?"

"Not a clue."

But he had. He was merely playing for time. Making these calls was detestable; he'd rather receive them. Then he could legitimately feel at the mercy of high and relentless authority. He diddled. He deliberately allowed himself to think of Maddy's cropped curly hair in the sunlight and his irrepressible need to touch it. Then hurriedly, almost like a rite of exorcism, he thought of the wife who had deserted him when they were twenty-four, after a year of marriage, and he gave a hasty touch at the pain which had persisted. Presently he dialed the number and waited for the ceremony of passage through secretaries.

The voice that addressed him at length was friendly and rather gay though absolutely correct; not by a decibel too gay or too friendly.

"We'll meet for a drink before dinner tonight."

Aidan said coldly, "I see no reason why I should go to that dinner tonight. It'll be a damn bore. I've made other plans."

The voice did not reply for a moment. "You're mistaken. I've something to say to you. I hear negotiations are coming a bit unstuck."

"Not to my knowledge," Aidan said even more coldly. "And I would know."

The voice laughed slightly. "No, you wouldn't. You see your position is exceedingly vulnerable since you are here openly but also in secret. Some want a compromise with Rhodesia, others want something much better. You've got to live with the two. In addition to this new nasty business."

"I can quit this job, you know."

He heard a click, as though a button had been pressed to close an open line.

"I doubt if you'd want to at this point." Then an enormously pleasant laugh followed. "I hear you had lunch with a bunny of a girl today."

"My God, are your eyes everywhere?"

"Oh, come, come. I was delighted to hear it because they've felt they had to keep an eye on her since she came. Her brother is not very cooperative. A spot of pressure on her may be indicated, I'm told, and you'd be an admirable administrator. I hate the business. I'm glad you're here."

Aidan felt an icy cold reach his heart. He could not trust himself to speak. Without a word he put the telephone into the cradle and sat staring at his desk, fighting the chill. Hardly a moment passed before the telephone rang.

The friendly voice, frozen along the edge, said, "I can't believe that that was a voluntary disconnection. Seven at L'Avenir? If I'm a bit late be patient. You will, won't you? Be patient?"

Aidan said, "I can't understand why a man in your position is so occupied with a man in mine."

The voice did not reply for a moment. "I don't altogether understand it myself, dear fellow. When things got unstuck in Salisbury the other day—well, never mind. You know what clever practitioners we are here of the *ad hoc*. I rather wish I didn't have such an expert reputation for it. Well, we'll have to make the best of it all, won't we?" He sounded tired.

Maddy got into the old car with the painted daisies and sank back with a sigh. Norman grinned at her again under his mustache, disposed of his legs and meshed the gears noisily as he watched for an entrance into the traffic. She relaxed under the sound and the smell of the car and of the daisies, though sunflowers and cosmos were more favored at home.

Norman said nothing as he fought with the traffic as far as the bridge, but while they searched for Maria Street he cast himself into a long discursive poem with broken refrains.

When he found Maria Street, he asked her what she thought of the poem and she said not very much.

"It's mine." He was not offended. "Twenty-five's the number? Holy Mother—look at it!" He jerked on the brake. "That's what's the matter! They put up a house like that eighty years ago when they had no vision and they've got no vision now and people don't burn it down. It's the slave mind. They haven't read the writing on the wall." He clutched the wheel, mildly obsessed, blowing on his long mustache. "So Maureen-girl lives there? It shows she'll be defensive. Don't let her think you mean to make trouble. You must take care about that. Shall I come with you?"

"Yes—no! What if she's not there?"

"Let's see how it shapes. Now straight up. All smiles."

The vestibule had clean broken linoleum. Maddy pressed a bell which read O'Connell-Dwyer. She heard the clatter of sharp heels on the stairs and the door was jerked open by a plump pretty girl.

"Well, you are—" Then her eyes opened wide and she shook back her long hair. "Was it you now who rang? I thought it would be my boy friend."

"You're Maureen O'Connell?"

"I am." The Irish softness in her voice was disarming.

"I'm Madeline Sayer. I'm staying at the Chesterton Place Hotel. I just want to ask you—" A motorbike roared up and stopped.

"Ah, there he is, the toad!" She made a clucking sound. "Always late. You're always late, Ted."

Ted said brightly without conviction, "Important delays. Got a kiss?"

"Never mind about that. Well, come on up," she said to Maddy. "Has the old place burned down?" The sweet softness in her voice did not change.

"No. I wanted to ask you a question." But she did not ask until they stood in Maureen's bed-sitter, where her roommate was drinking lemon squash and reading a film magazine. "It's about my brother. He told you, I think, that he was waiting for his sister—me—and that we were going to Scotland. Could you tell me anything else he said?"

The girl did not answer for a moment. When she said, "Why?" the word came out with a chill.

"He's disappeared. I got here on Thursday and haven't been able to find him. The manager acts very strangely."

Maureen said softly, "Why is it you think the man I talked to was your brother?"

"Well, were two American men waiting at the same hotel to take sisters on walking trips to Scotland?"

"That I cannot say. He was just talking about Scotland, isn't that so? He had—he had *come* from there."

"The man had come down from there? He wasn't *going*? Are you sure?"

Ted said suddenly to Maureen, "Old lady, it's time to push off."

She made a little gesture at him, but her eyes remained on Maddy. "That's what I said, didn't I?"

"Please tell me what he looked like."

"He was your age. Looked like you. But dark."

Despair surged in Maddy. The girl was lying. She did not know how to make her tell the truth.

"You're my hope. You're my friend. I'd never tell the manager if that's what you're afraid of."

"Afraid? What am I afraid of?"

"Yes, what's she afraid of?" Ted demanded, unzipping his windcheater, showing himself in tie and blue suit, fully able to look after his girl.

"I don't know. I *must* find my brother, Maureen. I *must* find him. I think you can help. What room did he have?"

Maureen's roommate had put down her film magazine and was sucking softly so she could hear.

Maureen glanced at Ted, and again shook her luxuriant shoulder-length hair. Her expression closed.

"Twenty-eight, twenty-seven, twenty-six—I don't just remember."

"Oh, please!"

"I don't just remember!" Maureen suddenly shouted. Then with a soft quick sullenness, "I'm sorry. You're vexing me."

"I must find him. I think you do know something and that you're afraid I'll get you in trouble. Please, I will not get you in trouble."

Maureen said in a low fury to her roommate, "Stop sucking on that thing. And you've got my pearl earrings on. I'll have them off you, you silly cow!"

"Maureen!" Maddy could not keep the anguish from her voice.

"My name is Miss O'Connell."

Ted, with great bonhomie and smelling of a hair conditioner, took Maddy by the elbow and eased her toward the door.

"She's a spitfire. I'll talk to her."

But Maddy drew away. Maureen was watching her hotly from under lowered brows.

"Miss O'Connell, I'll have to go to the police if I can't find my brother."

Ted gripped her arm. It was an inexorable grip. He held her so tightly against him that his windcheater rubbed against her.

She turned toward him. "You're hurting me." And then she saw, directly on a line with her eyes, the tieclip he was wearing. With all her strength she broke away. "That's my brother's tieclip!"

His hand went up swiftly to cover it. "You're a damn liar," he said. "You're a troublemaker. That's my own. If you come back, *we'll* get the police."

He thrust her so violently out of the door that she fell against the wall. The door was slammed and locked. When she regained her balance she ran down the stairs.

Norman, a notebook propped against the steering wheel, was writing swiftly. She ran to the car, wrenched open the door and sat close to him.

"What's up, love?" he asked gently.

"He's wearing Richard's tieclip. I gave it to Richard when he graduated from college. They lied to everything I asked."

"In that case, we go to the police." He shut his notebook, capped his pen and started the car. "A constable just went round the corner."

The constable, a tall young man, looked at them mildly, listened with his hands clasped behind his back, nodded, and said, "Come with me, miss."

Her story sounded wild and incoherent but he merely said, "Come with me, miss."

She scrambled out of the car and Norman cruised, with a few gaseous explosions, beside them. There had been no ambiguities in their responses; she had concealed nothing, felt no suspicions as she had with Aidan. There was no gulf fixed between them which she had been unwilling or unable to bridge.

As she stood behind the constable, he rang the bell. There was no answer. He rang again. He rang another bell and was admitted. He went up the stairs with Maddy behind him and knocked on the door. The silence was profound. He knocked several times and put his ear to the door. Then he beckoned, went ahead of her down the stairs. The basement door was locked. Shaking it lightly, he said, "There are back entrances to all these houses but I fancy they've not gone away. I'll be glad to force their door, miss, but first you'll have to make a charge. Will you do so? The police station is very near."

His manner was correct but there was a certain zest in his voice. She stood in the gloomy hall, frantic with frustration. The only sounds were the creaking of boards beneath their feet and the crying of a baby in the front flat.

"Oh, God—it *was* his tieclip!"

"Then make the charge, miss."

"You don't—I can't—it's terribly confusing. I'll have to talk with my friend."

"Police station is just in Elsa Grove, first left."

"You've been wonderful. Thank you. Thank you very much. His motorbike is still there."

"That is his motorbike?"

Norman was sitting on his heels beside the motorbike and rose slowly when Maddy ran up to him. "Look at those handlebars," Norman said. "Makes me feel tender. Look at the chopping. My brother had a Bonny like this."

Then he saw her face and looked at the policeman swiftly. "What's up, bird?"

"He can't get at them unless I make a charge. How can I make a charge? How can I say—"

"Get in!" Norman opened the door. "Thank you, officer."

He started the car noisily.

"How can I go into the police station and say 'a man at twenty-five Maria Street is wearing the tieclip belonging to my missing brother'?" Norman drove thoughtfully. " 'How long has your brother been missing?' 'I don't know.' 'You've not reported that he's missing. Why not?' " Norman looked at her. " 'Because I'm absolutely and utterly confused about what he's doing. Because I'm afraid I may hurt him, whatever I do.' 'Now just give us the known details about your brother, miss, and we'll make some routine inquiries.' And that's just what I'm afraid of, Norman. What if routine inquiries put him in danger?"

Norman parked the car by a cinema and did not reply for a moment. "Routine inquiries. That's the way your embassy chaps talk too, isn't it? They're all built right into the ground, rigid, no give—they'll never find him."

"Who will?"

63

"I'd say *we* might but isn't your brother rather built into the ground himself and mightn't it take quite a blast?"

After a moment she said, very low, "I hardly know what brother you're talking about. Everyone seems to talk about a different man. I have to keep telling myself Richard's *my* brother. Norman—" she hesitated and looked at him swiftly out of the corner of her eyes, "I think maybe he's a revolutionist." Norman stared at her with wide fascination. "Working for black nationalism. Unless Aidan was trying to set traps for me. Maybe he was. Why would he do that? That's what's so hard. I don't know these people. I don't know what's true. Maybe the embassy knows Richard's up to something and wants to ignore him so they won't get into trouble. If I go to them—" she started to laugh and fell to shuddering.

Norman pulled her ear. "Stop it!"

"Norman, I'm being acted on all the time—I want to act. What's the right thing to do? I can't afford to make a mistake. That *was* his tieclip. Maureen and Ted know more than anybody else—unless it's the manager. The police—"

Norman started the car abruptly. "We should have stayed by his motorbike." He turned and roared back toward Maria Street. Parking out of sight around the corner, he ran to have a look.

"It's still there," he said, settling behind the wheel again.

"What does that mean?"

"It means he'll not leave a Bonny by the curb all night. You don't do a thing like that. We'll wait."

"When he comes out?"

"We'll find a way to talk with him." He shot the car from the curb and parked where they could see down the street. "Watch that Bonny. I've got to study."

With a phenomenal dexterity he assembled and cross-referenced notes against the steering wheel, holding his pen between his teeth but discoursing nonetheless on human habitations of the future. She tried to cool herself by asking questions as she watched the motorbike. Some of his answers delighted him so much that he wrote them down in full. They talked about affection, friendship, sex and marriage as they related to revolution and architecture.

It was familiar and reassuring, far more real than the disappearance of a brother and the appearance of a tie-clip. An hour passed. People went by. Dogs on leashes and dogs free and sniffing went by. A motorist made a determined effort to park behind them and, when he failed, blamed the generation which rode in cars painted with daisies. The constable passed on the other side of the road. Suddenly Maddy caught his arm. "Norman—he's gotten on!"

Norman thrust all his notes onto the back seat and trod on the starter. They were behind the motorbike before it got well under way. But Norman let it go around the corner before he forced it to the curb.

The rider turned a furious face to the car.

"It's not Ted!" Maddy said with dismay. Norman faltered.

"Not Ted? Well, we'll find out what he knows."

He jumped out of the car. The boy, with long dark hair under his helmet and angry eyes, waited with his feet braced and his hand on the throttle.

"Bloody swine, what do you think you're doing?"

"We thought you were Ted. Where's Ted?"

"What the hell difference does it make where Ted is? I'll have the skin off you!"

"Okay. It was dirty. You've got the right. Where's Ted?"

"Please," Maddy said, "where's Ted?"

"What's Ted to you? I've got the right to ride this bike whenever he calls me—"

"Who cares about the bike? It's Ted. We must talk with him."

"Why? What's it to him?"

Maddy said, "He knows where my brother is. I've got to see my brother."

The boy pulled down his goggles and revved the motor. He raised his voice scornfully. "He called me to get this baby off the street. That's all I know. Stuff it." He shot expertly between the curb and the car and disappeared down the next street.

Norman shoved Maddy toward the car. "I don't like to say it, pigeon, but I think we need the police even if it makes a queer story. It's their job to sort out queer stories."

"How will they make Ted speak?"

"How will we, if he's gone to earth?"

"I'm not hysterical about police," she tried to explain. "I'm just cautious. I don't know what it opens up. I trust *us*. I don't trust apparatus."

Norman said only, "It's smart to know when to trust them. Shall we go right now?"

She sat miserably beside him, studying her clenched hands. He waited patiently. Presently he pulled her ear gently. After a moment she nodded.

The police sergeant was matter-of-fact and intelligent. He made an orderly array out of confusions. He questioned her carefully. He showed neither skepticism nor conviction when she told of "Martin Doer's" registration card and of the tieclip.

"It *was* his tieclip. I drew the design and a friend made it up for me."

He wrote this down. He wrote down names and addresses and the license number of the motorbike, which Norman had on a slip of paper.

"I'll send a constable now to twenty-five Maria Street."

"What else?"

"We'll check the license of the motorbike and the registration cards at your hotel."

66

"If it's been destroyed—? If they deny there was such a card?"

He was brisk. "Your word against theirs. We'll check hospitals again and send out a missing person's alarm."

Maddy hesitated a moment. "Do you believe me?" she asked.

The sergeant looked at her for a moment with a faint smile.

"I believe you're a young lady who's come to us for help and we'll do all we can to help."

"But do you *believe* me?" and now it was not so much a question to him as to herself. He seemed to understand this for he did not reply.

In fifteen minutes the constable returned to say there was no answer at 25 Maria Street. The sergeant reassured her. "We'll ask some questions when they come back. We'll keep in touch with you and you keep in touch with us." He smiled and nodded goodbye, raising a forefinger in farewell. It was humane and reassuring but her heart sank. She knew suddenly that real assurance must be far more subtle and profound. She stumbled as they came onto the street, and Norman caught her and looked at her with concern.

"Ill, pigeon?"

She got into the car and sat huddled for a moment. His wide green eyes did not leave her face, and he made no attempt to start the car. Then she grinned furtively.

"I guess I'm scared of the hotel now," she said with an effort at a laugh. "Maureen and the manager both want to skin me alive."

"Come on home," he said. "My Mum will look after you."

She suddenly smiled. He and George and Sandra had existed in a familiar disconnected fashion, going their own way. But he also had a Mum and a home and presumably a last name.

"What's your last name, Norman?"

"Powell," he replied with surprise.

"Your Mum wouldn't mind?"

"Why should she?"

She was silent for a moment and he kept his eyes on her as he turned the ignition key. The car moved very slowly as he waited.

"No," she said finally. "I'd better go back. It's where he can find me. But thanks very much. Thanks a lot, Norman."

"I'll give you our telephone number. You'll ring if it gets sticky tonight?"

"Yes."

She came into the lobby of the hotel feeling both nervous and resilient if blows awaited her. She passed the clerk without a word but he called her name. She braced herself but he merely held out a telephone message.

Call Jacques Bernard 734-2111.

Any name might conceal Richard or a message from Richard. The voice which answered was blunt and heavy.

"Hallo . . . Miss Sayer—hah! Are you related to Richard Sayer? Yes? I want him but I cannot find him. I will ask you to meet me at seven o'clock and I will fetch you at your hotel."

The Third Day
Evening

Jacques Bernard was not Richard, nor Richard's emissary.

He was a stocky, harsh-voiced Frenchman who offered his card with his greeting. Chief of the London Bureau of the French Press Agency, 14 New Bond Street. He looked down at her through black-rimmed spectacles. "Sayer is your brother? Then let us talk. Come along."

"Where?"

"Come and dine. Why should I wish to talk to you standing here in this second-rate foyer? If there is a mystery about Sayer let us unravel it in a civilized manner."

She was not as young as she had been two days before. She did not move.

"Is there a mystery?"

Now he looked at her sharply again and shrugged his shoulders ponderously.

"You and I," he said, "we both ask each other the same question." He smiled and for the first time showed a degree of charm. "I do not know your brother but he has inconvenienced me greatly. Oh, come along! I have a taxi waiting outside. Let us be hard with each other in the taxi."

He took her arm firmly and pushed open the door.

Someone was sitting in the taxi, as she discovered when she touched a knee, a man dressed in dark clothes, with a black face. His voice was not unpleasant as he said, "Good evening. My name is Jerome Nabuku."

Bernard violently pushed down a jumpseat and hoisted himself in, gathering his raincoat about him as he slammed the door. "Nabuku is a friend of mine." He turned around in the jumpseat with an effort. "He came to see me in the office today and I learn he is also a friend of your brother. Now what is all this mystery? A message comes from our head office in Paris on Tuesday that our chap in Lusaka says I must talk with Richard Sayer at Chesterton Place Hotel without delay. They do not condescend to tell me why, but before I can put myself into a position of service I find a message from your brother."

"When?"

"What is this? Saturday? Wednesday morning when I come in. My secretary says he will be in my office at ten. I wait till noon and then I call the hotel. They say he is not in. I leave a message."

"They said he was not in? They didn't say he was not registered?"

"Not in. I come around that night. The message is still in the box. I feel I have done enough, but this afternoon comes a red-hot call from Paris saying for God's sake send the stuff from Richard Sayer."

"When you called again today how did they answer you?"

"The girl says there is no Mr. Sayer but a Miss Sayer. Since both are Americans I make a bold move."

She was silent for a moment.

" 'Stuff from Richard Sayer.' What does that mean?"

Bernard's mammoth shrug could be felt if not seen.

"It seems he was acting as courier for our chap in Lusaka who is out of his mind because whatever it is has not reached us. Now our chap in Lusaka has vanished." He heaved, groaned and laughed. "Communication with Africa is distinguished by its failures. But my chief in Paris is making it easier for himself by saying that the key is in London." He hunched himself threateningly in order to open the door and struggled for change as he stood on the pavement.

He put his hands against the backs of his two guests and pushed them toward the restaurant as though he had often been tricked at the last moment. But he showed no further interest in the subject of their mutual concern until dinner had been ordered.

"Give me an educated guess." He looked sharply at Jerome Nabuku and at Maddy. "What did he have for me?"

Maddy thought of Aidan's statement that Richard was a "revolutionist."

Jerome Nabuku frowned and studied his companions briefly with small eyes of extraordinary blackness. "It could be anything, important or trivial. Important matters should not be handled this way. Your chief must be a fool."

Bernard thrust out his lips but did not take offense. Nabuku looked at Maddy for a moment and smiled faintly. "So he is your brother? I've got no reason to distrust him. . . . He was always honest and discreet." His eyes moved briefly to Jacques Bernard. "Mutti said we had to take chances with Americans like him. He would not have said that if he had not been reassured up to a good point."

Bernard lost his temper. "What is going on in your idiotic country? I sit in London and I am supposed to know why you chaps bait each other half a world away."

Nabuku's expression did not change. Impassive before, it merely hardened a bit now. "We are not baiting each other. Rhodesia is a horrid place for blacks. It is a country occupied by the enemy. Would you not do something about it?"

71

Bernard grimaced, then looked at Maddy for her reaction. He laughed briefly. "You're a pretty girl. That's good. Come on now, tell us what *you* know. Mutti is a great African leader—formidable, I agree. Can you add something?"

She laid out the bones of the desolatingly familiar story, so familiar that she could not see any disclosures that might endanger Richard. The only danger might lie in the fact that she was growing too accustomed to the situation and therefore unobservant.

She kept to the bones. The more alien Richard grew, the more urgently she felt the need to defend her brother. It was a fine point of metaphysics, this loyalty.

She did not mention the police nor her suspicions of the hotel nor the tieclip.

"What have you done about this potpourri of oddities?" Bernard asked impatiently. His tone stripped her of dignity and competence.

"The best I could. Nobody was worried but me. The bank and the embassy weren't worried, and when I found his wife—they're getting a divorce—she wasn't worried. No one was worried, just mystified."

Nabuku said sharply, "You are worried, I hope."

She looked at him without dissimulation. "Yes."

"So what did you do?" Bernard asked.

"Tried not to act helpless!"

"Don't you have any friends? Anyone you can consult?"

"No."

"That's absurd." He was impatient again; he even seemed to take offense, as though she were willfully asking for sympathy. His heavy black brows were drawn together over his black-rimmed spectacles. "Perhaps Sayer has a little friend."

"Perhaps."

"Perhaps your brother is hoodwinking you."

Suddenly she realized that she was very tired of trying

to outguess a world that had caught her unawares, tired of attempting to unravel a skein when she did not even know whether she held the first thread.

She did not know how to answer men like these, single-minded and powerful in their own right. She belonged to an entirely different world. These men would take what she knew and use it to their own ends. To them, Richard would be saved or expended according to the large forces they generated.

Were they different from Aidan? He lived in a world that overlapped hers—or so she sensed without knowing exactly what she meant, and he would know how to deal with these men as she did not. It was she who had to learn some special kind of wisdom in order to break through a fog that, as in nightmares, seemed without mercy or hope.

She felt these two were capable of coming out of the fog to trap her without the least effort on their part. And she would walk into that trap unless she took care. She should not have said she was without friends. That was very naïve.

Abruptly she excused herself and went to the Ladies' Room. She stood alone, leaning against the basin drinking one paper cup after another of water, wondering what she should do.

The awful realization that something had happened to Richard hammered again in her head. The police must be able to reach her! She thought wildly of going out of the restaurant without saying goodbye but her purse and her coat had been left at the table.

She came back reluctantly. "I'm sorry, but I can't stay. I have to go back."

Bernard patted her chair. "Sit down."

"No. I've told you all I know. It's—I must—"

Nabuku did not smile. He looked at her. "It's fright. We're

all confused—even this rhino here—because we don't know exactly what we're doing. Please sit down for five minutes and then I myself will put you in a taxi if you wish to go. You do not know us. Our credentials are not checked. Perhaps his look better than mine. He is frankly professional, a journalist who wants his story. He has joined forces with me because he is accustomed to working with experts. I am an expert black nationalist." As he spoke he was subjecting her to a scrutiny more penetrating than she had ever known before.

"Please sit down."

She sat down slowly, looking at neither of them.

"All but one of the Rhodesian black leaders have been scattered—like myself—or imprisoned." His voice was matter-of-fact. He made no effort to be conciliatory but his eyes did not move from her face, as though wishing to leave nothing to chance. "The one who went underground —Mutti—was a very big man. When your brother was in Salisbury two years ago, Mutti wished to see him. This came to me as a message later on. I do not know why Mutti wished to see him but we must all take risks. Let us say he asked something of your brother. In the early spring Rhodesia became an illegal republic, and the United States withdrew diplomatic recognition. Did your brother attempt to see Mutti after that? Only a colleague in Lusaka could tell us. It may not be important one way or the other. But I think we are all faced with something very big. I think so. I've had word that Mutti has been betrayed. If that is true he may not live very long. Torture is becoming explicit."

Bernard grunted loudly. "That was not on our teletype— about Mutti."

Nabuku said, "I think it is true. I talked to the Zambian High Commissioner yesterday. She is trying to find out. She has talked with her colleagues at the United Nations. It is possible they will ask for a Security Council meeting on

Monday because they have an immense documentation which must be disclosed."

"Waste of time!"

Nabuku shrugged. "Everything is a waste of time unless it works. You see, young Miss Sayer, why the situation is so compelling and why we are now asking questions of you?"

When dinner was put before her she automatically picked up a fork but her voice was without expression.

"Even if everything you say is absolutely true, I don't see how I can help. I've chased down every idea and everything is a blank." She looked at him with very young eyes.

"Tell me about Mrs. Sayer."

"She's English. She says she can't guess where he is. She says she hates politics but I don't think she thought he was in politics."

"I would like to speak with her," Nabuku said.

Bernard, who clearly had an expert attitude toward meals, impaled meat on his fork. "As I see it we know only one thing about Richard Sayer. He telephoned my office at nine o'clock and disappeared within the next hour. I suggest that the police be invited to examine this situation."

Nabuku said angrily, "You cannot go to Tory officialdom with a story about the Rhodesian underground."

Maddy said, "I have gone to the police."

After a moment Nabuku made an explosive sound and threw down his napkin. "Damn fool. Forget all about this conversation."

She nodded. "I see that's important."

"It's crucial. Do you really understand? *Nothing* must be said."

"I understand."

Bernard made a large noise of disapprobation. "A journalist is asked to join a political underground though he doesn't know A from B. What an idiotic age. Three men are missing. How are you going to find them, Jerome, sitting in London? Our agency man, your Mutti, her Richard Sayer." He raised a stentorian voice for the waiter. "Don't bother me with details. Just tell me when I have a story."

"I think one will bring the other two," Nabuku replied flatly.

Bernard had put her in a taxi, carefully counted out change for the driver, shook her hand formally, said, "Maybe we meet again," and slammed the door.

Nabuku had said nothing. He had merely nodded, unsmiling. Then he had suddenly looked at her with an observation so sharp that it came like a shaft of light. She had thought he was about to speak but the taxi moved on at that moment.

Intellectually she knew all about confrontations. At home she had played with confrontations. But now a door had suddenly opened and the summons of the darkness beyond was as real as a knife.

When the telephone rang it was Norman. "They've got your brother on the missing persons' list tonight on the radio."

"Good!" *Good*—she did not know whether it was good or bad for everything was moving into new dimensions and new demands. The strange man Richard Sayer needed some kind of assistance beyond her reach.

"Are you okay?"

"I'm okay."

"See you tomorrow."

Her instinct was as clear as a voice. *Don't abandon Richard. Don't go back on what you know. Can you stick it out?*

"Yes," she said aloud.

During the night she wakened suddenly and thought of her mother. Oh God, with a missing person's alarm some American newspaperman would get hold of her mother.

Though one o'clock in London, it was evening in Vermont.

"Darling, I've got rather strange news. Richard's missing. Yes, well, I'll tell you all about it in a letter. Everyone's busy on it—the embassy, the police—we've checked hospitals, *that's* okay. He'll show up, but I thought I'd better let you know."

"Maddy, Daddy's in California. I'll get a plane tomorrow!" Her mother's voice was as fresh and clear as though she were in the same room.

"No, no, darling. That's foolish. It's rather exciting, isn't it? Nutty Dickon. He always was crazy, wasn't he?"

"You're all alone, Maddy. You shouldn't be alone."

"I'm not alone. He's got friends."

"Have you called Cloris?"

"Cloris?"

"In Lusaka—wait, here's the number. Daddy and I'll talk it over—about me coming. Give me your number."

Maddy sat on the bed looking at her locked door. She had said *I'm not alone*. It was true with ironic variations. In a dark region of her imagination unfamiliar specters had form and substance, weight and measure.

She moved a table in front of the door and put a chair on top of the table. Yet none of this would protect her if she did not get clear inside herself.

The Fourth Day

In the morning she wakened with an odd sense of freedom.

Perhaps because the burden was being shared, merely that. The police knew, her mother knew, she was no longer stumbling around trying to find some kind of answer by herself. But she felt the relief ran deeper, something to do with herself growing up.

The faded chintz in the room had a sharp brightness as the sun crept along the wall. The barricade against the door formed a strong pattern. She lay for a time making angles with her hands to extend the pattern. Then she got up abruptly and took down the small barricade with some embarrassment.

To Bernard and Nabuku she was of small consequence. To Bernard, an expense-account item: "Dinner, six pounds," because Paris had idiotically confused its signals about Richard Sayer. To Nabuku merely one more pattern in a design of life and death.

As for the police, anything she found out must now be taken to them.

For the first time in three days she slowly, almost imperceptibly, let go. Maureen's rage did not bother her. And the police, large father-figures, would not permit the management to put her out.

As she waited for breakfast, she leaned out of the window to sample the day and then talked by telephone with Sandra, who proposed a *fête champêtre* of sandwiches and tea in a Thermos by the river in Buckinghamshire.

When the Scottish maid put down the breakfast tray she looked sideways at Maddy.

"The police came early asking for Maureen."

"Oh! Why?"

"I just wondered, would you have seen her yesterday?"

Maddy hesitated for a moment. "Is Maureen here this morning?"

"No. Though she should be; it's her day." The girl waited with her hand on the door. "It's strange, wouldn't you think?"

"I did see her." She hesitated again. "It's her boy friend, I believe—if the police are asking about anyone. He's pretty rough."

"Ah, yes. A lively fellow." She said it ironically, leaving Maddy unsure what her inflection meant.

The day was kind. When the sun disappeared there was no finality about it; it soon reappeared. George had a great many Sunday ideas which he enlarged at some length. Maddy liked the English words where they differed from the American and frowned as she grappled with Anglo-American imponderables which had never occurred to her before. Norman also talked a great deal in a spree of formulations and she roused herself, now and then, to take issue.

The place by the river had metal tables, a seasonal blooming of colored umbrellas and a few boats for hire. George arranged them in a boat and pulled off like a sculler into the river. But presently he tucked in the oars and they drifted, eating their sandwiches as the bank of alders and willows went past them dreamily.

Maddy trailed her fingers in the water and leaned far out to see what lay at the bottom of the river. She thought, in a sudden upswelling of heart, how merciful it was that she had found friends to whom she could speak even when the intonations were different.

She hunched against the side watching wisps and a dead bird and live swans with their cygnets go slowly by. She was glad that a powerful police was feeding fragments named *Sayer* into a large computer and reading the answers. If she slipped in *Aidan* what would they report? She frowned a little against her arm. Beautiful . . . but Norman was more real.

It was altogether a lovely day. George rowed now and then, taking them around curves in the river and then shipping the oars. When he rowed Sandra slept; when he sketched designs of water currents and floating leaves, she knitted. Norman asked to be rowed ashore, where he spread out books for his exam. Maddy slept and dreamed but could make nothing of the dreams.

No one mentioned her missing brother or Maureen or the police. That was the purpose of the day.

Toward evening, George said they'd have some supper and go to a film—American underground—that had just opened off King's Road.

Maddy said that she would like to stop at her hotel before the film, and ran in while Norman idled the motor.

Two messages were in her box. But far more compelling than a message was the long, slim, elegant, white-suited, beautifully coiffed, long-nailed, bracelet-jingling, angry Cloris who rose from a shabby chair.

"You've been away the entire day. Those two messages are from me. I asked you to keep in touch and you've not done it."

She came forward slowly and took Maddy by the arm, her thin fingers holding like talons. "It's been a maddening day, tied to my absurd telephone waiting for you to call. I've been here, in that impossible chair, for an hour."

Maddy glanced at the importunate messages, her insides stiffening. "What's happened?"

Cloris pushed open the street door and made certain that Maddy preceded her. "You didn't even take my five pounds. What was I to think? Why did you not keep in touch?"

"What has happened? Cloris!"

But Cloris was suddenly captivated by the daisied car, George's beard, Norman's mustache, Sandra's bare feet. She brightened and paused and looked very winning as she shook hands. Then she frowned, and jingled her delicate bracelets as though calling up her own spirits, and managed to create a small, rather elegantly ill-tempered scene by the car as she demanded that Maddy come with her.

"It's Modern Africa at the New Fortune Gallery. A private view." She spoke directly to George. "Her brother helped to put it together in Lusaka. A man will be there—*that's* what's so urgent." She frowned and seemed suddenly nervous or impatient, it was hard to tell which. "You've got to be there, Maddy. To meet him. Come along."

Yesterday when Maddy went to the police, she had made a promise to herself. Unknown men, uncharted plunges, must be met with the utmost discretion.

"Who is he? Cloris, I don't want mysteries any more. The po—" But she did not say it. She bit on her lip. "Who is he?"

Cloris's jaw hardened. She looked with a sudden sharpness at all this disestablished youth—though she herself was, chronologically, not very much older—smiled slightly and cut her words to their cloth. Though she spoke directly to Maddy she did not exclude the others.

"A man who knows Richard. A very important man. He can help but he's very starchy about his position. Any meeting has to be offhand. You don't look very smart"—then her charm flashed for a moment—"but you look very pretty." She turned to the others with her rare smile. "You understand why it is important."

Determined, arbitrary, illogical, anxious, she carried the day.

"I'll tell you tomorrow whether the show is worth seeing," Maddy said crisply to her friends.

The gallery was crowded. Long, narrow and uncomfortable, it had spent all its living on lights—experimental, resourceful, effective—and economized with burlap on the walls, no place to sit down and impossible ventilation.

No one was very smart, so Cloris need not have worried. Cloris, near-sighted, squinting slightly, said, "There's no point in trying to see the exhibit. I'll introduce you here and there and try to give you a sign."

Confronted with the backs of men's coats, the backs of heads, the textures of Zambian and Nigerian robes, the watery punch and despised biscuits, the roar of voices, Maddy waited in vain for a sign.

Cloris's charm had become warm and even dimpled. The elegance remained but the nerves vanished. "My sister-in-law, Madeline Sayer, Mr.—Sir—Lady—Lord—"

Suddenly Maddy saw Jerome Nabuku, in Western clothes, very black, with no grace but a large distinction. She made a spontaneous move but he looked at her as though he had never seen her before and she accepted the cue for what it was worth.

One of Cloris's friends introduced him as a Zambian journalist. "Lusaka?" Cloris asked. "But why didn't I meet you before?"

"Because I am penned in London," he replied, charm irradiating, looking at Cloris intimately with wide-open eyes. For the next five minutes he gave the appearance of a man captivated, relishing her acidulous witticisms as though each were a banquet, while Maddy waited for the sign— the sign!

Suddenly she felt a hand reach for hers. A black hand. Nabuku had disengaged himself and was directing her unobtrusively to the stairs, which had a rope tied across them.

He lifted the rope and said, "We'll sit here for a moment. The stairs are not very comfortable but they're private. Now laugh quite a lot because I have serious things to say."

He sat on the step below her so that his head was on a level with hers and she saw the black thick skin, the yellowish eyeballs, and felt the great power of the man.

"I must tell you first that was a very dangerous man she introduced to you at the last."

"Which one!"

"Low and smiling," he said. "Mr. Gerald Claverton. Did your sister-in-law bring you here? Why?"

"To meet someone she said could help Richard."

"She meant Mr. Claverton, I believe. He is not a friend. He is a killer."

Maddy turned her great brown eyes on him. "You've got to be kidding!"

Nabuku shrugged slightly and placed her small hand on his large palm. "Shall I give you a brief lecture on Rhodesian liberation, little one? There is nothing winsome about getting your freedom when your enemy has all the power. This killer, Mr. Claverton, has never lifted his hand, I'm sure, and has no real need to do so. You'll find no killing on his record, but he encourages a deadly legislation. He represents the antiblack party in the Foreign and Commonwealth Office—though of course there is no record of such a party—and his position as a Parliamentary Under Secretary permits him to manipulate policies by the most simple expedients: he can delay a file until it's no longer needed or he can interpret and define a recommendation so that I, for example, would scarcely recognize it. A brute force nearly always operates behind diplomacy—for both sides. You don't like that? Well, there it is. Claverton is pro-Ian Smith to such a degree that I am astonished he is not a liability to any government in power." He reflected. ". . . Because he's so able, he probably disguises it very well."

Maddy said nothing. A painting in raw reds and yellows was in the line of her vision. It had a terrible vibrancy and assaulted her mind. The troubled currents of liberation movements versus established opposition had blown on her college campus but she had never stood directly in the high wind before. With a sudden urgency she turned from the raw reds and yellows and studied the black face as close to her as a lover's. It did not tell her very much because she was not equipped to read very much, but she sensed that he was a sad man and a hard one. She sensed this in unfamiliar ways.

"I will not bore you," he said, studying her in turn with a slight smile. "But if you are concerned for your brother you should have some knowledge of where he lived in his mind and his work."

"How do you know where he lived in his mind?" she asked, watching the crowd below, as impersonal as a school of fishes swimming in the complex and urbane lighting.

"I told you last night I trusted him—as far as I am able to trust a white man. Look at that wood carving over there. What does it say to you? Do you like it or not? You're willing to reserve your judgment. I too. That's my feeling for your brother."

She frowned.

"It's a matter of justice." Nabuku studied her as he leaned against the burlap wall. "Four and a half million black people cannot be tricked and despised by a quarter of a million whites. That is twenty to one. The world has no room for such discrepancy. If Africans trick and despise each other that is bad enough but the other is worse. You agree?"

He was smiling and watching her. She nodded, observing

a black woman with a beautiful and intricate headdress move smoothly through a network of bodies.

"We have now a permanent division of land in Rhodesia by which the whites have the richest and largest and best—no nonsense about ratio here. The polarization is being carefully legalized and within a year we will have apartheid, though perhaps another term will be used. We will have it, that is, unless something is done."

"What?"

"Our friends at the United Nations won't let anything happen in a corner. That is good. They've got files of maimings and tortures which we hope cannot be set aside when we make them known." Then he looked at her as though he could barely tolerate her youth, her inexperience, her educated beliefs. "It is a prerevolutionary situation I'm told by a white politician in Salisbury, and he thinks the next step is violence. He calls it a collision course with destiny. What do you think of words like that?

She had been staring at him, and now turned away to follow with her eyes a black man in a blue robe who was trying to make his way without spilling his punch. She said as calmly as she could, watching the blue robe, "My brother?"

"He is a very good American who has archaic faith in the ballot. But he knew we did not have even the old-fashioned chance of a ballot unless we made it impossible for Salisbury to refuse us the vote. And I think he knew that our courteous political efforts in the past were as helpless as children's games and that we must have a strong base that is respected. And that men who carry guns are respected by men who believe in suppression. Of course he is not a revolutionary, your brother; he is a nice young American who loves Africa and believes in simple truths. Does that sound like him?"

She smiled faintly. "I've heard him described by three different people . . . none sounds familiar."

"You do not think he has disappeared because he is a nice discreet young American?"

She looked at him very troubled.

"What are you trying to tell me?"

His half-smiling glance traveled over her face.

"How will you take this kind of stuff to your embassy? Or to the police? It will tie their hands. We are much more likely to find your brother because this is our business and our hands are not tied. But then on the other hand"—he brushed the sleeve of his coat as though finicky details were important—"I may be preparing us both for surprises. I was your brother's friend because people I trusted said to trust him. Should I trust the party of the first part or my reliable suspicions?" She suddenly disliked him very much and her expression showed it. He laughed slightly. "In Africa trust is not a natural virtue. It's not a spontaneous growth from the slave trade or colonialism. If I use you, that may teach you how to use me, and Richard may be the gainer. How do you like that?"

All the natural virtues swam through her mind. She shook her head. A great modern totem, massively restated by the lighting, alarmed her imagination for a moment and she did not try to answer him. He touched her hand lightly.

"Cheer up, as you say. I think your sister-in-law is looking for you. Isn't she pretty? Though I don't believe black men really have a taste for blond ringlets. Please look happy! If Richard Sayer is on our side we are on his. Now your sister has turned aside, but guess who is approaching you? Claverton. Well, I've told you all I can about him. He knows who I am just as I know who he is. Perhaps you had better keep clear of us both."

She saw that the man identified by Nabuku was making a courteous path through a group in the doorway, pointing and smiling at her. She was swept by indignation and helplessness and turned hotly to Nabuku.

"How? Just tell me that? *How* do I keep clear of you all?" Nabuku shrugged playfully as he rose.

Claverton stood with one foot on the bare wooden step and bowed to Maddy. Then he held out his hand to Nabuku; smiling and silent they shook hands. Maddy made no effort to move but she observed Claverton with a sharpness born of necessity.

He was tall, slender, his impeccably smooth hair an undistinguished greying brown, his eyes concealed by his spectacles, his nose thin, his mustache modest, his clothes not very smart.

He said to her, "Mrs. Sayer is looking for you. I believe she wants to leave." Maddy stood up slowly. Nabuku bowed slightly, nodded to Claverton and disappeared into the group by the door.

"I'm to keep you here so she does not lose you again." A killer? His voice was extremely pleasant, even gay. "I've persuaded her to allow me to give you both dinner. Is that agreeable to you?" He made it sound very agreeable.

"I'm—are you—?"

"I discovered only a few moments ago that you are Richard's sister. I can't tell you how pleased I am."

The Fourth Day
Evening

She went with them to dinner, on fire with attention, caution, efforts to extend her capacities beyond anything she had dreamed.

The restaurant was small and, in Maddy's terms, elegant. Elegant it undoubtedly was, in chartreuse and silver, the waiters' jackets a dark green. The menus were as large as placards, the name spelled across the chartreuse cover in silver: L'Avenir, Bruton Street.

The Future. There had better be one.

Claverton and Cloris paid no attention to her after the order was given, and she was left to observe them and the place as she chose.

Nabuku said he was a killer, but who is Nabuku?

Her instinct was to believe Nabuku because he was black and she a nineteen-year-old politically liberal American university student. But a strong natural honesty obliged her to get as free of all preconceptions as possible.

It was not easy. Just one reliable objective fact would make it easier. The only objective fact, however, was Richard's absence.

Her dislike of Cloris grew as she sat there ignored. It took on a fine edge of contempt. Cloris had managed to suggest that she, Maddy, miniskirted, short-haired, was merely a kid, inexperienced, easy to rule. It was done casually, with an iron hand, reducing Maddy to seething impotence.

As Maddy watched Cloris lean gaily toward Claverton, arch her shoulder, jingle her bracelets, she thought wrathfully that Cloris would never raise a hand to help Richard unless it helped herself. And this man, this man—this dark-suited, neat-haired, eyeglassed ornament of the Establishment, who had created the impression of friendship without using the word, was as trapped by Cloris as Richard had been.

Then something quite strange happened. Though Cloris remained very unreal, jingling and arching and smelling sweet, her expression frozen except for a pinpoint of light which showed in her eyes when she glanced at Maddy, he, Claverton, began to change as the meal went on.

After the sweet, when the coffee had been brought and Cloris had gone to tend to her ringlets, like the focus of binoculars being adjusted, he began to swim into view. It was not simply his nose or his mustache or his skin or his conservative necktie which underwent change. It was the man himself. His smile became shy and charming. He took off his spectacles for a moment and laid them beside his plate and his eyes became gay and full of life. His voice became soft and took on an edge of humor. He gave the impression of seeing her for the first time.

It was a remarkable tour de force. She found herself smiling back, thinking, "Now it's coming—Richard," waiting with a sudden expectancy as though everything had been moving to this point.

While he stirred his coffee and the new persona steadied before her, he looked at her. "Richard is a remarkable young man, really first class. I think you should know that because

Cloris doesn't understand how highly he's regarded by the men he works with." His smile lighted his face. One might trust him for the same reason one trusted an absolutely charming chord of music.

"Are you one of those?"

"I have that pleasure."

L'Avenir was so discreet and soothing that one was scarcely aware of people at the next table.

"But he's an American and you're a British—what are you?"

"Oh, one of those odd British factoti called a Permanent Under Secretary. I don't work with Richard in my official capacity but we all have many interests in common."

She frowned and looked at him. "You're using the present tense. When did you see him last?"

Then he smiled gently and resumed his spectacles.

"The other day."

An explosion took place in her head. She tried frantically to grasp the pieces. "The other day—where?"

He looked at her a little the way Aidan looked, as though seeing her clearly, as though knowing that she was real, bright—and anxious. He even laughed at her slightly but in a way that would never do harm. He leaned on the table toward her, with a deliberate employment of charm that she was too busy to appreciate.

"I want to say something to you before I reply." He drew in his chair slightly so that someone might pass. "Now listen attentively because you must understand. I'm very fond of Richard. I think he's uncommonly gifted. I should like to see him go to the top. He would if he were an Englishman. With the American system, I'm at a loss. It's a terrible pity if he's wasted. You know, it's rather—"

"Where is Richard!"

The glint behind his spectacles could have been annoyance or it could have been amusement or it could have warned her. He hesitated as though temporizing with these choices. After a moment he took off his spectacles again and rubbed his eyes.

"Richard's all right. He is for the moment detained." He lifted one hand and let it fall on the table. "By black Africans. So I'm told."

"Why couldn't he send me a message?" Her heart was pounding with a mixture of relief and dismay.

"Perhaps he did and it's not been delivered. These people are not always adjusted to amenities."

"Where is he?" She desperately needed to narrow this conversation to something concrete.

He studied her for a moment, quietly, not alarmingly. "I had hoped that *you* knew."

She did not really believe him but she was too inexperienced to know how to play out this role. "If I knew I'd do something," she said in a small flat voice, not taking her eyes from him.

Charm disappeared and the dry pedantry of the man took its place.

"I doubt if you could do anything alone against the kind of people who are holding him."

"I don't believe it," she said very low. "I don't believe it. You know where he is and he *can* be gotten at."

Claverton did not reply for a moment. Then he looked at her and replied very gently to the point he was forcing at her, "You don't truly know what you are talking about. If they want what he has badly enough these people become savages again."

Nabuku had tried to say something to her when they sat on the stairs and she had not understood. Now she tried to reach back and examine it. But she was not conditioned to distrust a black man. She would have to remember precisely and examine with absolute care, and she could do neither in this hermetic, fashionable room that was essentially alien to her.

Her eyes were on the empty cups but in a moment she

looked at Claverton, hoping against hope that she would somehow possess enough understanding to read what she must in his face. Kind, watching her with concern, eyes a bit guarded behind his spectacles, himself shuttered, the focus deliberately blurred, he said, before she could speak, "This is very hard for you, but I felt I must tell you all this. Perhaps I should have asked Cloris first—"

She shook her head fiercely. "Cloris doesn't know me."

He said rather shyly, "What *have* you done, if you know nothing?"

"Not much." She did not look at him. "I went to the embassy—and the police. And—and I called our mother."

"In the United States? Good child! I daresay that was wise. I see Cloris has met a friend but she'll be returning in a moment. I will say something quickly, and for that reason indiscreetly, but you and I both care for Richard and that is all that matters, isn't it? You have something that will insure his safety."

"*I* have?"

"What do you have from Richard?" he pressed her.

"I don't know!"

"You received something from him recently?"

"Only letters and cables." He smiled and nodded. "But there is nothing—"

"If you'll read them carefully, I think you will understand what I mean."

"But what—what! And how do you know?"

He did not reply, or show any signs of replying. Glancing toward Cloris, he seemed to judge the degree of her pre-occupation and said, "The police and the embassy, alas, are no help—and I don't believe your mother can be of much assistance either. But a quiet offer for Richard's release could, I think, be negotiated within twenty-four hours if you will cooperate like a good little one."

All calm and caution left her. Even resentment. "How?"

He frowned slightly. "Why—act on one of his cables."

"Which cable? What does it say? Why are you being so evasive?"

He looked at her and said quietly, "The bank."

"Oh! I tried—but the bank manager said there was no emergency."

"There is an emergency now."

"But how can I prove it?"

He put his hand on hers. "Give me the key like a good child and I'll show you if you'll come with me."

Her throat was dry, her hands were wet. This was not the way to convince her! "You *do* know where he is!"

After the briefest hesitation he made a deprecatory sound. "I suggest you use the key."

"But it's just his will!"

Claverton shrugged.

She wondered wildly if he could see the key to the deed-box burning through her purse. She thought at the same time of Nabuku's suggestion that round was square and oblong triangular in this world where gentlemen could be killers in a struggle for power.

Claverton, watching her intently, said with impressive authority, "You're obliged to help. You have no real choice since we both wish to help Richard. Think about it while you're sleeping." He patted her hand. "I'm sure if your mother were here she would advise it strongly. We'll dine again tomorrow night. Here is Cloris."

Since Maddy was no fool she recognized an official position in his elegance, his careful sentences, above all in his authority, though it all lay as raw material in her mind, inchoate, and virtually unusable.

Cloris, smelling very sweet, was full of apologies. She glanced quickly from one to the other with her periwinkle eyes but showed no desire to ask questions. Claverton said he was terribly sorry to hurry them but he faced an evening of documents.

Maddy was not listening to him but to the things in her

head. She stumbled over an unexpected step and was furious with herself for stumbling. He caught her arm and held it.

"Take care! Stop dreaming, do. I'll take you home on my way." His grip was very tight. "In you go."

She sat in a corner of the taxi, thankful for the dark. Cloris rustled beside her, her delicate scent filling the narrow space. He said something to Cloris which seemed to please her very much. In his light, pleasant voice he gave the driver directions and added, "A charming dinner . . . thank you both very much."

He took out his cigarette case and Maddy saw Cloris's profile in the flame of the lighter. She also saw that his eyes, behind his spectacles, were fixed on herself. For that moment she saw an expression so strange that it could only be a trick of the uncertain flame. She stared at him until the light went out.

The traffic was heavy, the taxi did not move for long intervals. Maddy thought *This man . . . this man—Nabuku warned me against—but who is Nabuku?* The need to know whom to trust and whom to distrust was a stone in her mind.

Since she had chosen to trust the police she should put this into their hands. But *this* was a high official of state and he might be able to work only in quiet ways—*if* he were honest. If—if! If he were not honest could the police or the embassy reach as high as he in the available time?

If oblong was triangular and black and white interchangeable she needed a dispensation of wisdom that, in this tomb of a taxi, was nowhere in sight.

They reached Cloris's flat first. As Cloris brushed Maddy's cheek with her lips she whispered, "Trust him. He's got all the wires that need pulling."

Maddy did not reply. She watched Claverton walk with Cloris to the door and lean down to kiss her.

So that was that. But kissing was cheap.

When he rejoined her he said with the trace of a laugh, "It's jolly important to trust me. How old are you?"

She was startled and began to reply but pressed her lips together instead.

"Come along," he said gently, "how old are you? Well, never mind. The point is, you *are* up against something that needs far more experience than you have. Shall I bring you a letter from Richard, telling you to fetch his papers from the bank?"

She found her voice. "You mean you do know where he is?"

He did not reply for a moment. "How persistent you are," he said.

A measure of boldness came into her voice. "Let me see him. Let *him* tell me."

He turned his head sharply. After a moment he said with a small cutting edge, "My area of negotiation is very limited. I doubt that would be considered. . . . Of course, I can try. But how much longer do you want to keep Richard in pain and distress?"

She caught her breath. "What are they doing to him? You *have* seen him!"

He made a vexed sound. "My dear young lady, I'll tell you for the last time I've been drawn into something very much against my will to help a man—a white man—I admire. I am at a considerable disadvantage and you are not making it easier."

His stricture should have made her compliant but it did not. Whether from perverseness, stubbornness or self-will she pressed the question: "How did you know Richard sent me a cable?"

"From Richard himself." He looked at her. "What a distrusting little creature you are."

"What is in the box at the bank that's so important?"

"My dear, that's what no one has told me. But you've tried

to open it, so I assume you know. In that case it's no surprise that Richard trusts you to get him released."

When she did not answer he turned his head and said coldly, "You're being self-willed and that's terribly stupid under the circumstances. You're behaving like an ignorant child and Richard did not expect that."

His arrogance disturbed her more than his words. A man who spoke in that voice was totally outside her experience and might be capable of any of that mysterious influence which is supposed to lurk in the halls of the powerful. She might be terribly ignorant but she was also terribly anxious to know right from wrong.

I can know! For a dismaying moment she thought she had spoken aloud. But she had said nothing and continued to say nothing, not knowing what words to use. He stirred and sighed, and then, as though aware that the silence had to be broken, by him, with authority, he said, "Richard has put his safety in your hands. In your hands. I'll call for you tomorrow at seven thirty."

"What proof have I got that you can do something?" she cried. "Nobody gives me proof of anything. Maybe this is a trap for you and me both!"

"I'll ask for a letter from Richard to give you tomorrow evening."

She stood for a moment in the hotel lobby and then knew she could never sit alone in her room. Uncertainties swarmed in her like desperate children trying to get over a wall. She came back onto the street where she was, at least, not alone.

Walking in the lighted dark, her hand on her bag where the bank key lay, she thought *I want Aidan.* Perverse and childish, perhaps—yet he stood halfway between the familiar world of Norman and the unknown world of Nabuku and Claverton.

Aidan would not be lost in either world. He had a quality

like Richard. He was Richard's age. She groped for other reasons.

Early in the morning should she go to the bank? If they still refused her access should she go to the police or the embassy, without mentioning Claverton, and make them force the bank to open the box?

Right this minute, what was happening to Richard, wherever he was? With terrible resolution she had to cut down her imagination, but images slithered around like mercury. The rain was falling lightly but she scarcely noticed it. Presently she came to a pub and went inside because she was cold and did not want to be alone.

She took out her key ring to which she had added the deedbox key.

Richard also had a key. If he was being tried beyond his limits why hadn't he surrendered his key? Unless of course he had lost it and was helpless and this key *would* turn the lock....

When Aidan answered the telephone he heard the charming arrogant voice.

"So sorry to bother you but things are coming a bit unstuck. It is absolutely imperative that she cooperate, absolutely imperative. He's left them no alternative. But she's not cooperating. She's acting like a stupid child. And you, alas, are the only one with a hope of influence."

Aidan did not reply for a moment. "She's acted, in the last few days, like a brave child. How do you know she won't go to the police?"

"Use your wits, dear chap. What can the police do?"

Aidan was silent. Then he asked, in his slow deep manner, "Why are you risking so much? What do you want that Richard has?"

For a moment there was no reply. "What do you know about little or big?" The voice became very clipped. "This girl has to cooperate. For her brother's sake. And hers. And ours. It's very tiresome and I'm very sorry I got into it. But you're in it also, so I'm forced to leave this part to you."

"No!"

"Oh, yes. We have no choices any longer, my friend. Stupid, if you like, but that's how it is."

"I refuse."

The sigh was gentle but remained imperious. "Then let me tell you: Mutti is being held. Perhaps you know that but you don't know his life isn't worth a farthing unless they get what they need. They're relentless. You understand what that means, I'm sure." Some of the charm had returned.

"What could be important enough to tempt a government to kill a prisoner with the whole world looking on!" Aidan's dismay was in his voice.

"The whole world? Dear chap, only the Security Council."

Aidan said violently, "Why do you think you can coerce me?"

"Ross, by now too much ambiguity's involved for you to disengage yourself without damage. Perhaps we've all been misguided but it's too late to think about that. Sayer is almost prepared to force his sister's hand in order to protect Mutti."

"Let me talk to Richard!"

"You and she both want to talk to him." The voice sounded weary and even, Aidan felt, a little afraid. "Would she believe you, if *you* took a message from him?"

"Why should she?"

"Extraordinary situation . . . Well, let me know after you've lunched with her tomorrow. By the time I've dined with her she should be—"

"I promise nothing," Aidan said curtly.

"Oh, yes, because you must."

The pub was not a consoling place. Its dark shining

woodwork and old-fashioned lights were high camp and they depressed her to such a degree that she sat with her head lowered. One or two of the kids were half wrecked. As she tried to remember some of the things Nabuku had said to her, she felt that their protest was as irrelevant as the hussar's jacket on one of the boys. Wake up, she whispered. This is life and death.

Nabuku had said Claverton was a killer, and Claverton had suggested that Richard was held by black Africans only a generation away from ritual knives.

Here in London, in this city of ordinary people, an African struggle affecting the world was going on and in some fashion she and Richard were at its center.

If she did not know which way to move, right or left, she did at least have to keep a single mind. In the gregarious and open world in which she had lived there had always been someone to talk to if she were caught or confused. Now she was totally and imperatively alone, having to accept a responsibility she could not even share with her mother.

. . . Then she had to grow up for the occasion.

She knocked her knee painfully as she rose to leave this place which had nothing to give her, nothing whatever.

It was raining when she came out.

By morning she had to know exactly what to do and she could not afford to make a mistake. She shivered.

As she came to the steps of the hotel she heard her name spoken. In the light from the open door she saw Aidan, the one person she had not dared to want.

She ran under his umbrella and caught his arm. "Oh—did you know—?"

He said, smiling down at her, his voice warm, "What?"

She laughed shakily. "That it's nice to see you."

"Good. You're wet. Get a coat and then walk about a bit with me in this beautiful rain."

"Oh, yes. Come inside?"

"No."

She felt wildly excited, close to thankful tears, as she put on dry clothes and found her raincoat. As she changed her shoes she measured the time she had known him, a day and a half, and added to that her feelings when last she had left him, half dismayed, wholly bewildered.

But because it was more natural for her to trust than to distrust she let the avalanche of events—the tieclip, the visit to the police, the dinner with Nabuku and Bernard, and the strange disquieting world which Claverton had opened before her—settle the question of caution and trust. She *had* to trust him and she was honest enough to know why: because she wanted to.

When she came out of the hotel he was still standing on the steps where the light from the door fell the length of his raincoat. She slipped her arm in his. He smiled down at her and said nothing. She liked his quietness. Most people made too much noise.

"Everything's happened," she said. "Where should I begin?"

"With you—what you've been doing."

She had not permitted herself to look starkly at what Claverton had said: that Richard was being held in danger and pain. Now she began to face it pragmatically.

"Having dinner with a man named Claverton—Gerald Claverton. Do you know him?"

Aidan did not reply for a moment. "A rather grand bloke?"

"Yes."

"He's in the Foreign and Commonwealth Office." He added after a moment, "Very high up."

"Do you know him?"

"Well, it depends on what you mean by *know*."

She sensed his glance, heard the tightening in his voice.

"He says Richard is in danger and pain. He says he can negotiate his release." Putting it into words made a terrifying demand, for now she had to believe or not believe.

Aidan did not respond in any way. They came to a street intersection and he did not wait for the traffic.

"Can he?" she asked after they had walked another moment or so. "Is Richard in danger and pain?"

"I don't know." His deep voice sounded very far away. After a moment he asked with an effort, "Did you believe him?"

"It was the most concrete fact yet—what he said—absolutely the only thing I have to go on. But why didn't he go to the police if what he says is true?"

"Because of his position, I suppose. It's very high."

"Why are you limping?"

"Limping? Oh. That's nothing. I fell off some machinery years ago. It bothers me when I'm bothered."

"Could it be true—what Claverton said?"

"Madeline." He looked down at her. "We've both known Richard might be in danger. Have you done anything? Talked to anyone?"

"I went to the police. I—I talked to my mother."

His expression was unreadable. He considered her for a moment, his dark brows drawn together over dark eyes. He started to speak and then turned away.

She persisted. "What do you know?" He hesitated for so long that she shook his arm. "What do you know about him —Claverton—more than his official position?"

"He's an expert on African affairs."

"Like Richard?"

"Far more sophisticated."

Each question had been answered only after a long pause. The impression was like a dream or a slow film.

"How did you meet Claverton?" he asked at length.

"Through Cloris. She said he could help." She stopped abruptly, drawing at his arm. "I also met an African named Nabuku. He said Claverton was a killer. For God's sake, help me! Who is right? Can Claverton help or is he a killer?"

He continued to look down the dark street where lamps and car lights caught the fall of the rain. He did not stop walking but he said very low, "Go to the police again, and the embassy—and clear out. Let them find Richard if they can. Get out."

She stared at him. Presently she whispered, "Who are you? Why are you really in London?"

He turned his head slightly but he looked at the pavement, not at her. "I've told you."

"You haven't. . . ."

"Listen to me." He took her arm and drew her against a building where there was some protection from the rain. "I have not lied to you. If I can negotiate an agreement for a large company my father owns, it will break an impasse between Salisbury and London, and the government at home will cooperate on something much more important. The thing that's more important involves black leaders here and at home."

"How can you mix up negotiations? You have to lie to one or the other!"

For a moment he shook her arm violently and then he shook his head almost as savagely as he turned away. "No. It can be done if you keep your eyes open all the time."

"I don't believe it!" She struck his arm but he did not look at her, merely moved away slightly. "You *have* to make a choice. Everyone does in the end. Your father and business security—and negotiations. I'm scared of negotiations. Richard isn't negotiable!"

His face was very white when he turned toward her.

"Is that what you think—that Richard is being used somehow in my negotiations?"

"I don't know. I don't know anything except that every time I feel I can trust you something happens that tells me I can't!" The great brown eyes were frantic in the little pale face as she tried not to look at him. "What do I know except my brother is missing? I've talked to no one but strangers. I don't know any of them. That French journalist may be a fake—that Claverton may be a killer—or he may be my best friend. All I know about you is what you've told me. Like a fool I paid too much attention to *wanting* to trust you, wanting—oh damn! The only people I should trust are the police and that fool at the embassy. I want to get out of the rain."

She turned up her collar and left the protection of the building. He caught her arm.

"No, I want to go back. I'm perfectly all right, thank you. I'll make the police make the bank let me have what they've got, and I'll have dinner with that man tomorrow and see what he's offering and make sure he can deliver. I'm not afraid for myself—just for Richard. I'll negotiate too. I'm the only person I trust."

"You'll do nothing of the kind." Aidan gripped her arm painfully. "You'll trust me and wait."

"Why? So that Richard can't talk any more and you'll get a signature on a paper?"

His eyes blazed. She thought with a sick excitement that she had never seen anyone so angry. He tried to speak and then he turned on his heel and left her.

The excitement carried her almost to the hotel and then the tears came. When she ran past the receptionist she was not attempting to control herself. He called her and she shook her head. Before she reached the lift he had caught up with her. "It's a wire, miss," he said, staring avidly at the tears.

She nodded and tore the envelope open as the lift rose.

MEET ME AT THE MOUNT ROYAL, PRINCES ST., EDINBURGH 11 AM MAY 16 DICKON X.

X was the old code for *keep it silent.* Not even her mother knew.

May 16 was in one hour.

103

She lay on the bed, her face pressed into a pillow, trying to think.

If the wire were from Richard then both Claverton and Aidan had lied to her. She had no reason to trust Claverton, but if the wire were true Aidan was deceiving her.

In this terrible quagmire anything might be true and anything false, and Richard's survival depended entirely on her ability to distinguish the true from the false when both looked alike. Dickon X.

No one could possibly know what that meant except Richard and herself.

She roused herself and sat on the edge of her bed staring at the carpet. Is the wire true?

She *could* know what was true—somehow, somehow not be fooled.

Presently the trembling lessened and she went to bathe her face in cold water. The wire was a happening and she had to respond. At least it allowed her to act. She assumed there were no more flights to Edinburgh that night, but the only place she wanted to be at the moment was the airport.

She made sure she had her passport, all her money and the deedbox key. She took nothing out of her bag or the closet so that the management could not accuse her of running out on her bill. When she passed the reception desk the clerk was nowhere in sight.

A mistake was possible in anything she did, but she believed there was more truth than falsehood in "Dickon X."

If it was panic that was sending her in the middle of the night to the airport—panic that she might miss the first plane in the morning or panic that Aidan or Claverton might stop her by some sort of black magic—then she must live with the panic until she had laid it to rest. But she felt very calm and this suggested that something other than panic had made her decide.

At the terminal she found that a bus was just leaving for a late flight. She went aboard and sat in the rear.

In the waiting room she found an obscure bench, took off her shoes, curled up her legs and tried to stay awake. It seemed an action both wise and alert but presently she fell asleep with her head against the back of the seat.

In the middle of the night she sat up with a very clear course of action. But it faded immediately and she fell into sleep again.

With the dawn she wakened with a start and stood up in confusion. When she remembered where she was she put on her shoes, determined not to sleep again.

She booked on the first plane for Edinburgh and then found a buffet for breakfast. After a time she walked outdoors and tried to decide what to do about her mother. . . . At eleven A.M. she, Maddy, would know about Richard and that would be time enough to send a cable.

When the plane for Edinburgh rose from the runway she had a relentless grip on her calm.

The Fifth Day

Edinburgh was grey and beautiful.

She reached the Mount Royal Hotel (which was on the schedule Richard had sent her) just before ten o'clock. The wire said eleven. The reception desk was up a flight of stairs. She went up the stairs and asked the clerk if Richard Sayer had a reservation. The clerk fiddled with cards and shook her head.

Okay, okay, she stilled herself. But restlessness ran through her like an electric charge. She could not imagine any way of sitting in the cream and leatherette lounge for an hour without exploding in a thousand pieces.

The doorman was a leathery, long-nosed, crinkle-eyed fellow with a soft Scottish voice. He told her this was Princes Street, those were the public gardens across the way; that was the Scott Memorial, over there; like a watch above the city, was the Castle. "Beautiful, wouldn't you say, miss? Oh, it's a grand city. I'm thinking there's not another like it in the whole world. Mind the traffic, miss. Now then, wait till it's clear. There you go."

She stared up at Sir Walter Scott in his majestic cavern,

took a small turn among the eagerly blooming flowers in the public gardens, studied the names of the donors on the iron benches, lost herself for some minutes thinking about the castle above the city, against the low northern sky. Then abruptly she shook herself. She was capable of only one thing at a time in her life. She was made for immense and single absorptions. Now it was Richard and eleven o'clock.

She ran and ducked through the Princes Street traffic. The doorman shook his head fiercely and his soft voice rose harshly.

"It's because it's nearly eleven," she said. "Has any man come into the hotel since I left?"

"The laundryman," he said, still shaken by the risk she had taken. "And a fat chap carrying his own case."

She ran up the stairs and went again to the reception desk. "I'm waiting for Mr. Richard Sayer, who will be registering here. Please show him where I am—right over there."

The woman clerk, black-haired, thin-faced, tight-lipped, nodded without speaking but watched sharply as Maddy sat in a low chair by an unused ashtray facing the stairs and the desk.

Her heart was beating fast. A woman got off the lift with a bag and went to pay her bill at the desk. A florist's assistant surrendered a box to the hall porter who disappeared into the lift. A man came up the stairs and went to the desk.

Maddy half rose though she was close enough to see that the man was not Richard. As the electric clock above the hall porter's cubicle jerked toward eleven, she went to stand near the desk. Her ears were ringing, her throat was dry.

The hands of the clock jerked to the hour. She thought, *My God, if that man kills him in London because I came to Edinburgh I will never forgive myself.* But she had some sort of conviction that she had not made a mistake.

It was five minutes past eleven. Her throat was very tight and her stomach had fallen away.

She would wait till a quarter past eleven and then she would have to make some decision. And the right one, the right one, the right one.

At ten minutes past eleven the clerk leaned across the desk and called her name.

"Miss Sayer—Miss Sayer—the telephone. Take it in the hall porter's room."

She ran. It took her a moment to find the telephone and another moment to realize she was saying, "Yes yes yes!" into silence. "Please, please!" she cried desperately.

The clerk's voice answered her. "He rang off! I told him to wait—that you were right here—that I'd fetch you."

"What did he say?"

"He asked that a message be given you. He said he was your brother Dickon. He said plans had changed—that he could not meet you until the Station Hotel in Inverness. Hold on, miss."

But she did not hold on. She put the telephone in its cradle and went out to the desk to confront the clerk, read her expression. Maddy's reaction was an awful despair that truth had been snatched from her hand.

"Was it a young man's voice?" she demanded, holding onto the desk.

"Well, now, that's a question, isn't it?"

"American?"

"I should think him to be so, wouldn't you?"

"I'm asking you!"

"He sounded very pushed. I'm thinking that's why he did not wait. I said, 'Hold on, she's right here.' Then he said that about the Station Hotel in Inverness and I said, 'Hold on, please' and then I called you."

"Did he say when I was to meet him in Inverness?"

"No. He sounded just pushed. Oh, it *is* too bad. I *am* sorry."

Maddy turned away. She tried to smile. "You did what you could. Can I get a train to Inverness?"

108

We'll rent a car in Inverness and get camping equipment.
"Yes, yes, the hall porter. Jock, this lady—"

Jock said a three o'clock train left from Waverley Station at the end of Princes Street. Maddy went to the lounge and sat with her back to the clerk and the hall porter. Go back or go forward? Let her mother know? Let the police know? Simply call the London police and ask if they have any information? Return to the London bank and do what Claverton told her?

The X after Dickon's name in the wire had not been used lightly, she felt sure. If he were in danger and asking her help he was also giving instructions. Four hours by train to Inverness. Two hours by air to London. In London an embassy and a police were trapped by routine unless she could provide them with something more substantial than fears and suspicions. In London Claverton was obscurely threatening, Aidan unknown and thus more alarming than anyone else because she needed so fervently to trust him.

From her bag she dug out the schedule Richard had sent her. The Station Hotel in Inverness. There it was. Each time that a development coincided with a detail in Richard's letters, she felt steadied, as though given an inner direction.

If she could sustain the initiative, not be tempted by red herrings to right or to left, she would have the best chance of finding the truth. And finding the truth meant finding Richard.

But how did one recognize red herrings or truth?

One *can* know the truth, she whispered. That's the purpose of truth—to be known.

Her thoughts swept up Claverton and Cloris and Nabuku and the boy with the tieclip and the hotel, but she turned away. Somehow they were all wrong. Aidan . . . She longed to believe but did not dare. Then words he had said came back. *See the police and then clear out. Ask them to talk to Claverton.*

That made sense. Aidan had emerged for a moment with

perfect clarity. She would telephone the London police and then she would go to Inverness. She drew a deep breath and stood up. This was acting, not being acted upon.

In the narrow airless telephone booth, she heard the call being put through to the police station in Lambeth. The sergeant with whom she had talked was not in. "Has he had any word about my brother? Anything from the missing person's alarm? No? Then please listen carefully to me. I was told last night by a man named Gerald Claverton, in the Foreign and Commonwealth Office, that he knew where my brother was and could negotiate his release. I don't know whether to believe him." She heard the duty sergeant click his tongue.

"Miss," he interrupted her, "I can't take such charges on the telephone. You'll have to come in, talk to the detective on the case."

"I'm calling from Edinburgh. I can't tell anyone any more than this. You're the police, aren't you? You can talk to anyone, can't you? Can't you?"

"Miss, I don't know who you are. You'll have to make such charges in person."

"Please. My brother *is* missing. Talk to the American Embassy, Mr. Burgess." She took a deep breath. "Tell him what I've told you. Tell him to call my mother. Here's the number. Are you writing it down?" He was. This he could do. Then, "Talk to a fr—a man, Aidan Ross—wait a minute—" If this call was a terrible mistake, the consequences were now out of her hands. Holding the phone against her shoulder, she searched for Aidan's telephone number. "The number is 444-9284. Will you follow it up—please. Please!"

"All I can do, miss, is turn it over to the detective in charge."

"How soon?"

"As soon as he comes in. Within an hour."

She drew a deep sigh. "Thank you."

Putting up the phone she stood for a moment in the booth, her forehead against the door. What else? One could go over details again and again until they had too much meaning or none at all.

Richard had said *Inverness,* but if she left some token of herself a link with Edinburgh would be established. Leaning on the hall porter's desk she wrote Richard a note saying where she had gone and why. "Just in case," she said to the clerk, "there's a mix-up and he does come to the hotel after all."

The clerk with all her thin intensity and perpetual frown was ardently sympathetic. She patted the envelope, with Richard's name in block letters, and said, "I will—I will. I'll see to it. Now it's a long time till that train goes. There's a wee bit of Edinburgh you can see if you'll walk. Right round back is just the New Town. Very beautiful. Not new a bit."

The Georgian houses and leafy squares of the New Town were an antidote to too much waiting and wondering. The day was gentle, the streets were harmonious, the traffic calm; Richard loved Scotland and she understood why. When she at last fetched up at Waverley Station, London had faded; she was convinced London held no answers.

The station was cavernous and terribly shabby. She sat in a cramped buffet eating a sandwich and listening to gentle voices that suggested a world susceptible to some kind of order.

She studied the grimy counter. Her call would force the police to take a few more steps. They would certainly get in touch with the embassy. And the embassy would pull strings.

If Richard were not in Inverness. . . . She shook her head. Under her breath she hummed, "*I live one day at a time, at a time.*" Her restlessness had returned and was like a nervous dog on a leash. If she let it go free she would not know how to control it.

111

She walked up and down the crowded station, stopped at a magazine kiosk and bought a magazine which she forgot to take with her, bought a road map of Scotland which she did not forget, watched two children chase each other around a bench until they vanished after their mother. Then she saw it was a quarter before three and ran to the Inverness train where she waited with mounting impatience in an empty compartment until three o'clock.

By the time the train started, a youth had joined her, reading a sporting sheet except when he stared at her.

When he continued to stare she walked up and down the corridor and tried to force an interest in the housing developments and the car cemeteries outside the city. But when the train left these behind and ran through open fields, she returned to her seat, determined to practice some element of faith by attending to the green and wooded land that might be Richard's sanctuary.

But the young man did not take his eyes from her.

She opened the map and spread it and Richard's schedule on the seat beside her. She circled the towns on his schedule and found they made a straight course to the north.

The young man continued to stare. He could see the map. He could easily reconstruct where she was going. With too much haste she tried to fold the map and then had to refold it correctly and put it in her bag. Glancing at him she saw him drop his gaze and fumble with his sporting sheet.

If he is following me—if someone has set him onto me—I don't know what to do. Appeal to the conductor? She had not seen a conductor. Lock myself in the washroom?

"Why are you staring at me?" she asked suddenly.

For a moment she thought he had not heard her. Then he made a grimace, wiped his hand across his face and applied himself to his sporting sheet. But after a moment he looked at her over the top.

"Sorry. I was told to watch out for my sister's girl friend

and I was puzzling my head were you her. You're not her, are you?"

"No."

"Well, maybe I'd better go look. Bye-bye."

She could not afford to be such a fool again. Her reaction doubled her against her knees in nervous spasm. The waiter, coming through at that moment with his tray of cups, studied her sharply. "What you need is a cup of tea, miss, for that heaving stomach. Here, take a cup, and the pot'll be along in a minute. One shilling with a biscuit."

Waiting with the empty cup she talked to herself without pity. "You see something and are frightened because it looks like a man or a tree or a bear. Then you look again and see it's just a trick of light. Even the way it looks changes then, and you can scarcely remember why you were afraid. Yet you'll be afraid again unless you stop fooling yourself."

When the tea came she refused it and took out the map. This time she simply held it between her hands like a talisman as she watched the sky and the countryside, fighting to get herself put together.

Above deep glens the mountains rose, snow on their crests and yellow gorse on their slopes. In the fields, hungry seagulls formed a white carpet behind the tractors as the earth turned, and little rivers curled through the meadows where lambs and sheep lay, a dozen crows resting with them.

Maddy suddenly did not want to be alone in an unknown land.

Norman showed up at the Lambeth police station just as Maddy's train was pulling out of Perth.

"*She's* vanished now and what are you going to do about it all?"

Even when they told him that she had called from Edinburgh he sat with his knees spread apart, his elbows on his knees, and shook his head stubbornly.

113

"You're not doing enough. There's something more you could be doing."

"Such as what, young man?"

Norman continued to shake his head. "You've got to think like she did—forget your routine—" He put his head in his hands and was not prepared to give way.

"Do you know a friend of hers—Mr. Aidan Ross?" the detective asked.

A faded photograph "Inverness, Capital of the Highlands" faced Maddy across the compartment. She wondered where Richard had telephoned from, whether he had called from Inverness or whether she would have another stretch of waiting and wondering in Inverness.

She thought that the thing she had to do without fail was to keep alive the intuitions which had no pragmatic measurement. Everything else could deceive her, intuition alone had been trustworthy. When she saw this clearly enough she would know what to do when she needed to do it.

It was the best she had and it must serve her.

Beyond Pitlochry she came under the spell of the moors and of the low, cloud-filled sky, which in retrospect became the sign and image of the Isles.

Two old ladies came into the compartment at Kingussie, smiled, nodded and talked in Gaelic with great sallies of laughter, watching her with occasional sharp fond glances as though the compartment gave them certain responsibilities.

They did little to relieve her forlornness but she got pleasure from listening to their soft voices speaking an unknown tongue not only very fast but very low like a brook purling.

When the train finally reached Inverness she followed the old ladies onto the platform, where they nodded, smiled and said goodbye.

She asked the ticket collector for the Station Hotel and

he said she'd just turn to her left when she left the station and there it would be, wouldn't it?

The small baroque hotel lay with an indisputable elegance in the curve of the little station square. Life in the square came and went swiftly. As Maddy ran up the steps of the hotel, car doors were slamming, the square was being quickly emptied of automobiles, and by the time she reached the lounge the granite soldier in kilts, commemorating Highlanders killed in Egypt and the Sudan, had been left in solitary command.

Inside the door she hesitated, getting her bearings. The reception desk was at the far end of the lounge which widened into small parlors to the right and into a gloomy corridor on the left. A broad, curving and handsome staircase rose to the upper floors and windows looked down on the lounge from galleries above, while light flooded the stairs from a glass cupola at the top of the building.

At the reception desk she asked for her brother. The clerk, a girl with long hair, said after a businesslike inspection of forms that he was booked for that evening.

Maddy gasped. She had *not* been fooled. The young clerk watched her for a moment.

"It's such a wonderful surprise," Maddy tried to explain. "I wasn't absolutely sure he could make it. May I have a room near him?"

"He's booked for eighty-one. Eighty-five—will that do?"

"Oh, fine, thank you."

"Second floor."

She escaped to the lift, where she embraced the walls, danced and talked aloud during the moment of its ascendancy. "Richard, you fool! Oh, Richard!"

Booked for this evening. It was close to eight o'clock. She was hungry. She was not hungry. She was restless. She was calm. She searched for Room 81 before she put the key into 85. She put her hand on the door; she even knocked on it

115

for good measure. When she stood in the middle of her own room she rocked and stomped ceremoniously with an invisible Richard.

Her only possessions with which to establish a claim to the room were the key and her purse. With a touch of ritual she centered them carefully on the table by the bed. Then she plunged her face in cold water, combed her hair, put on fresh make-up, counted her pennies and decided against dinner tonight. She knocked once more at Room 81 since he might have arrived in the ten-minute interval. Hearing nothing, she went down to the lounge and sat facing the door.

Maddy waited for several hours.

It was a long wait because her hopes had been high.

A waiter brought her some milk and a sandwich. The hall porter told her that the last train from Edinburgh came in at nine. The last plane from Edinburgh came in at ten, unless it was late. The hotel was closed at eleven.

The chair she had chosen was soft and opulent. At nine thirty she moved to something more austere to help in the fight against sleepiness. Because her legs dangled she drew them under her. Oh Richard Richard Richard Dickon.

To the hall porter she looked such a child that he consulted his heart to know what to do. When, at ten thirty, he came over to speak to her, he hemmed and hawed.

"It may be he was driving. There's a real mucka mist below Slochd. Verra coarse weather for driving. And the plane—well now, I don't know. . . ."

"After eleven how does one get into the hotel?"

"Well now, it's verra closed then, but I'll not be locking before eleven and a quarter. I shouldna fret. There's a load of time."

She nodded and wanted to thank him but thanks were confused in her head with exhaustion. Putting her head against the back of the chair she fought against sleep and the deadly uncertainty that had dogged her from the moment she left London last night. Last night? A thousand years ago! Eleven and a quarter, she thought with an awful relief, meant she could sleep, Richard or no Richard.

After a time she walked to the window and back and into the parlor to turn the pages of *The Scotsman.* But the chair was her fortress. She returned, curled up her legs and tried to keep her eyes open.

She dreamed of Norman. Rousing herself she longed to hear his common sense. Fumbling in her purse for his telephone number she started to laugh; silent laughter shook her whole body.

She had telephone numbers for all the people she feared but she had lost Norman's number.

As she was gasping with her suppressed laughter a man came through the street door. Her heart leaped. Dear God— dear God—

The hall porter had taken a sheaf of papers to the desk and was engaged with the clerk. Only Maddy was near enough the door to reach out, to half rise, half call, and then to fall into such silence that even her breath was held.

For the man was not Richard, as she had first thought. He was Aidan Ross.

Richard would be following . . . she had to give herself a moment to think . . . Richard was slamming the door of a car and coming in. . . .

But there was no man and no car.

Aidan was an emissary from Richard. She started to call, "Where is Richard?" for Aidan must have had some contact with Richard in order to know where she was. Then her strange, metaphysical agreement with caution made her move instead to the shadow of the stairwell. Wait . . . wait just a moment.

She heard the hall porter's voice as he approached.

"She must have nipped up to her room, sir, just before

you came. She's been waiting for you the whole evening, a right worried lass. Very glad you've come, we all are. Here's the lift. Room eighty-one. Good night, Mr. Sayer."

Leaning back in the shadows she heard his deep voice saying, "Thank you. Good night," and then the lift rose creakingly. He had passed himself off as Richard. No emissary. A trickster.

She went up the stairs slowly and sat on the top step for some time trying to take stock of her situation.

Somehow she had been tricked. For five days she had had nothing but shocks and this last shock was almost too much.

The loneliness of the sleeping hotel chilled her. Shakily she got to her feet and looked down through the gallery window at the grand staircase and the lounge where she had spent the whole evening. A single night light cast deep shadows.

Why not simply unlock the front door and get out? Into the dark square? Sit up all night in the station?

The station was probably locked. Everything in the town was probably locked except the police station.

Take refuge with the constables?

Where would that get her in her search for Richard? She pressed her forehead against the window and dreamed of bed. She could not think or trust herself until she had some sleep.

No sounds had come from the corridor. Aidan might come out at any moment to go to the bathroom, and the last person she was capable of meeting was Aidan. She ran past his room and fumbled with her key. It took an eternity to unlock the door but when she was safe she locked and bolted it.

In the dark she took off her clothes and crept into bed.

Out of a deep fathomless sleep she was summoned by a small persistent sound. When at length she sat up in the dark she realized that a steady knocking at the door had wakened her.

Her first impulse was to respond. She put her foot on the floor and half rose but then she caught herself. Aidan. She knew it was Aidan. He had perhaps been knocking for some time since the knocking soon stopped and she heard footsteps going down the corridor.

She lay dreadfully wide awake yet unable to move. The wind was blowing a can down the road with an awful racket. In the faint light from the street she watched the curtains stirring. Several streets away a dog barked.

Presently the sound came again, a gentle knocking. Then a low voice called, "Maddy, Maddy!" She moved silently to the door.

Hardly breathing, she stood against the wall. After a moment she heard another sound, a soft *whish,* and realized that a letter was being pushed under the door. She did not stir for an eternity, not until she heard the retreating footsteps and then she still waited for a space longer.

Even after she had picked up the letter she sat in the dark, holding it between her hands. When she turned on the light she looked first at the signature. *Aidan.*

He said briefly, "I must see you. Something urgent has developed. I will meet you at seven o'clock for breakfast."

The question flooded over her again. How in God's name had he known where to find her?

If the police were searching for her they might, with patience, have located her name on the flight roster to Edinburgh, but Aidan would certainly not have been able to do this in a few hours.

Then she remembered that she had told the sergeant in Lambeth that she was calling from Edinburgh. It would not take long to check hotels, or for the Mount Royal receptionist to remember that she was going to Inverness.

If the police had given Aidan this information, either deliberately or inadvertently, it suggested that they might be working together. That meant he could be trusted. Or did it? The police had talked to Aidan only because she had urged it. Perhaps they had uncovered his black guilt and he was in flight.

The more she struggled for a sensible answer the darker became the night and the deeper her wonder.

The Sixth Day

It was six o'clock when she woke. The light outside deceived her; she thought it later and dressed hurriedly.

An unfamiliar hall porter presided in the lobby; the receptionist had not yet come on duty. Maddy said to the porter, "I'd like to call one of your guests about breakfast. Will you connect me?"

He groaned because he was struggling with a bundle of newspapers. "What room, miss?"

"I don't know. Mr. Aidan Ross. He came in late last night."

He consulted the registration. "There's no such name down here, miss. The last name"—he leaned over and peered closely—"is Richard Sayer, Room eighty-one." When she did not reply he looked at her. "There's no Mr. Ross."

This was what she expected but her anger blazed. "Thank you. I must have made a mistake."

Why! Why did he impersonate Richard! She could find no answer that was not monstrous.

She walked out of the hotel into the elegant square because it was impossible to stay in the same building with Aidan until she knew exactly what she meant to do.

Whether she turned east, west, north, south was of no consequence. She moved like a piece of machinery.

For the first time she forced herself to question seriously whether she had been tricked into going to Edinburgh. Dickon X. It seemed the one irrefutable fact that could not be explained away.

But if Richard had been forced to send that wire, had been compelled—he was in pain, Claverton had said—to make a wire foolproof, had used Dickon X under pressure or threat, then the childlike creditability of the Dickon X was smashed forever.

Was she getting too close to the truth in London? What truth? That Claverton was *not* an enemy after all? That negotiation *was* possible? That she had made the fatally wrong move?

The tears were running down her cheeks. A traffic warden looked at her sharply and watched after her for a moment. She was only partly aware of her tears. When she had to blow her nose she roused herself.

Inverness, the capital of the Highlands.

She should be in London. She should be fighting with all her power to make the police act, the embassy act. She should be talking to newspapers, storming Ten Downing Street and the White House.

You get so involved in the dilemmas, so trapped in personal labyrinths, so committed to the interpretation of experiences that you cannot extricate yourself or separate cause from effect until you abandon the whole damn mess and begin afresh.

Inverness, the capital of the Highlands.

Refuse to be frightened. Refuse finally and irrevocably.

Perhaps she said this aloud. In any case she turned and ran back the way she had come.

I have to love Richard enough to stop being afraid.

Running up the steps of the hotel she turned toward the

dining room. Aidan, busy with eggs and toast, was the first man she saw. He put down his knife and fork, rose and stood silently leaning against the table, and they remained thus for a moment or so, looking at each other. He half smiled; his eyes were very searching and did not leave her face.

After a moment she shuddered and sat down.

"What will you have for breakfast?" he asked.

She shook her head. Nevertheless he gave an order for rolls and coffee and then leaned back in his chair watching her.

She was as silent as he, as intent on examining him. . . . *Finally and irrevocably refuse to be frightened.*

"How did you know where I was and why did you pretend to be Richard?"

"Because I sent the wire to you signed Dickon and because I telephoned the Edinburgh hotel, sending you on to Inverness."

She said, "Oh!" and the tears came into her eyes.

"Stop it!" he said softly. He laid down his napkin and stood up, found her bag and hung it from her shoulder, took her arm and held it tightly till they reached the street. Then he put his hands in his pockets and walked with his head down, stonily, to the castle grounds.

She walked beside him, regretting the tears but shocked, nevertheless, by the truth.

He stood for a time looking down at the River Ness as the wind lifted his dark hair across his forehead. She sat on a bench struggling to make sense out of shock. Presently he began to walk slowly up and down in front of her, limping slightly, and she was obliged to watch his remarkably expressive face and the formidable reserve of his manner.

A pigeon hopped close to him and he paused for it to get out of the way, but when it moved he did not resume his pacing. He sat down beside her, staring at the river and the low clouds against the pale sky and at the long romantic row of houses across the river.

"I sent you the wire because it was the only way to prevent you going to Claverton. He is the enemy. I tried to tell you this in London but you would not believe me. I had to do something. Claverton is a paradoxical and desperate man—as desperate as a man like him ever gets. But he thinks faster than the rest of us and has many advantages."

She said, "Where is Richard?"

"To the best of my knowledge he is in London."

She jumped up and started across the grass. He caught her.

"Sit down. For God's sake, sit down. I'm sick and tired of you not trusting me!"

"Why should I?" she asked hopelessly, refusing to sit down.

"Sit down." He pushed her onto the seat. "Claverton is anguish and disaster. Will you tell yourself that like a litany? Claverton is anguish and disaster."

"I've only got your word for that!" she cried.

"That's enough." He turned his head fiercely. "You must understand—that's enough. My word is enough."

"You said one thing and then another in London. You contradicted yourself. I don't dare *not* be suspicious."

"Richard is my friend."

"That wire was signed Dickon."

"He's my close friend. He talked to me about you. I knew what you called him. I knew where he meant to take you. I have to act for him but I cannot if you behave like a fool."

"If you were his friend you would have given me some proof that I could accept. You've never done that. You're not doing it now. If he's in London I should be in London. I should be tearing the place apart."

He watched her moodily from under lowered brows. "I can't offer any proof except my word. But you will not go to London." He did not raise his voice. "If you go to London, they'll have two of you." He stood up abruptly and caught her by the shoulders. "For God's sake! I can't give you any proof. You have to trust me. You have to trust someone. Richard is my friend. I'm his friend. I'm your friend."

He turned away and paced out a square. "Madeline, you've got things moving. You jarred the police when you telephoned from Edinburgh. A friend of yours came to see me, a young chap with a red mustache. The police asked if he knew Aidan Ross and he came around jolly quick. He'll make a bloody nuisance of himself with the Lambeth police, thank God. I told him I was coming up here, and why. I told him to keep on making a nuisance of himself."

"Norman—"

"Telephone him. Perhaps he'll persuade you. You didn't tell me about the tieclip but he did. They've not found the chap wearing it, but they're alarmed, I promise you they're alarmed. There is nothing else you can do in London. Do you understand me?" He stopped in front of her. "There is nothing else you can do except keep out of danger." He hesitated for a moment. "They want you so badly they'd go to great lengths to get you."

"Why! Why do they want me?"

"You've got something they want."

"Yes. Yes, I have access to a deedbox. I can use it to negotiate."

He took her arm and obliged her to sit down beside him on the bench.

"*You* can't negotiate with these men. You wouldn't know how to begin. They would simply manipulate you against Richard. If Richard will not tell them where his key is— and I know the pressure they're putting on him—no, wait! not a slow fire under his feet but sleeplessness and endless questions—if Richard won't give in, he would be horrified if you did."

125

Maddy had grown very white, but he continued relentlessly. "Had you thought about that? Yet you were willing to give in. You're the one who can't be trusted not to break. As long as he doesn't give in, he's safe. If you gave them what they wanted they would destroy him, as a witness against them. And probably destroy you too."

She looked at him wildly, color flooding back into her face.

He was implacable. "I'd rather have you on my side than anyone I know. But you're a danger now to Richard. You're a danger. I'll keep you away if I have to do violence."

She sat very still. Finally she said, almost as implacable as he, "What do you know? I think you know everything. Maybe I'd trust you if you'd tell me."

He took some moments to answer. "I have very few facts. I've not seen Richard. I've asked to see him, but I've been put off each time."

Maddy said very quietly, "Has it occurred to you that maybe they don't have Richard at all?" He looked at her sharply.

"No, it had not."

"There's a lot of mental manipulation going on. Maybe that's what they're exploiting—what I don't know and can't see. Maybe they're using all kinds of fears and assumptions and ignorances against me to get what they want out of me. And Richard is really hiding someplace, not able to get in touch."

He was frowning. She sensed the same immense control and withdrawal that she had felt in London, but this time he did not abandon her. "It's possible, isn't it?" she asked.

He said, "Yes," with an effort. "But not probable, because of Claverton. Although Claverton is very rattled right now, he has not made a false move. If he were in the dark, he'd expose himself to all kinds of false moves. As far as I know he has not seen Richard—he has not opened himself to any kind of charges if the whole thing explodes in his face—but I think he knows exactly where Richard is and what is going on. He's immensely skillful. I don't know what the pressure is on *him*, but the stakes must be very high."

She said quietly, "If I am in danger why aren't you?"

"Because I don't have what they want."

She leaned forward against her folded arms. "How did you get involved?"

"One day I found I was inexplicably dealing with Claverton's office on this Rhodesian proposal. The next day—last Monday or Tuesday, the ninth or tenth, I've forgotten which —Richard's name was mentioned for the first time. Richard had been indiscreet, they told me. I knew him well, didn't I? Would I help to get him out of the fix he was in? I was very cautious and asked for details, which were not given. When Richard did not meet me for lunch on Wednesday, I tried in my own way to find out what had happened, but they began to press in a manner that was immensely adroit and formidable."

"They?"

"Claverton's office—which really means Claverton himself. I don't think his secretaries knew what the ambiguous memos meant, or the very skillful telephone calls. There was never anything overt—except that my original talks faded away and no one seemed to know why."

She said slowly, "I think we've got to go back to London. Make them tell the truth."

"No. The police can't *not* find out now."

It was very hard for her to give up.

"You think you're abandoning him?" he asked gently.

She nodded.

"Tell yourself that the only thing we know is that we know nothing. The police will have to do the work."

"Will they?"

"My God, I hope so. I'm counting on it."

"But I must have some responsibility!"

"Keep yourself intact. That's your responsibility." He stood up suddenly. "Richard meant to rent a car in Inverness and take you to the north. That's what we're going to do. We'll go to exactly the places he planned and perhaps pick up a clue."

She sat without stirring. "You don't really believe that," she said.

"I think it's as good a course as any. And safer than most." He held out his hand. She stood up. All she really knew at that moment was that she could not be alone, not because she was afraid but because she was exhausted.

"Why are you doing all this?"

He was going slowly ahead of her down the castle path. With one of his rare smiles he turned. "Because of you. Richard. Mutti."

Her heart swelled. "Shall I believe that?" she asked, running to catch up with him. He put his arm across her shoulders and kissed her lightly.

"Yes."

She hesitated for only a moment. "All right." Then matching her steps with his, she said, "Why did Claverton tell me black Africans were holding Richard?"

"Because he's a master of obfuscation. Because he's got a colonial mind. Feel free to conjecture."

She turned her head away.

"You'd like to cry," he said.

"No!"

He put his arms around her and she wept.

At the first garage Aidan rented a car and drove back to the hotel through the traffic of cars and bicycles hooting their way to work. "I'll pay the hotel bill," he said. "Don't stir. I'll be back in a minute."

She had no desire to stir. She felt she could never stir

again. As she waited, with eyes closed, fatigue and loneliness became so intolerable that she was willing to let them go forever.

She did not see him run down the steps of the hotel, and she was startled when he wrenched open the car door and hurriedly backed into the square.

"Something happened in there."

He smiled and shook his head. It was a test of faith. She was sure something had happened but she did not press for an explanation. She sat very still as they crossed the bridge over the River Ness. He glanced at her and read some of her thoughts. "Everything we do in life is a risk," he said lightly, "for truth—against lies. This is just one of those risks."

She smiled faintly and roused herself.

"Are you all right?" His voice was anxious. "You look very white."

"I haven't slept properly for a long time."

"For God's sake, get in the back and sleep. I'll rouse you at Bonar Bridge and show you the true Scotland."

"How do you know the true Scotland?"

"My grandparents were Scots. I lived with them here while I was in school. This is my childhood."

She nodded. When he stopped the car she climbed obediently into the back seat. He rolled up his jacket for a pillow and she was asleep before he came to the turn in the road.

He was perfectly honest. He knew he had been absolutely honest. He had held nothing back. He glanced in the mirror and saw only the mound of her hip in her scanty skirt and resolutely thought of her as a child. His relief was profound. He would keep her in Scotland until he knew she was safe.

"It's very strange, isn't it," her voice came sleepily from the back of the car two hours later, "how little we know about anything."

"Oh, life!" he said, taking a steep-backed bridge casually.

"I want answers." She sat up and drew in a deep breath. "Where are we?"

"We're coming into Invershin."

She combed her cropped hair and put on some lipstick.

"I'd like to come in front with you."

He stopped the car but she did not come immediately. Instead she stood for a moment beside a little river. All the Scottish rivers she had seen were uncommonly beautiful, swift and alive. When he joined her they walked up the bank.

"I spent my vacations with my grandparents here," he said, stooping down to put his hand in the racing water.

"Here? Invershin?"

"Sutherland. Richard and I became friends when he heard that my grandparents had an old house of whitewashed stone above a loch. In the summer it never really gets dark. When I was a boy I stood in my window at midnight and watched the mares play with their foals in the half-light."

She sat down on the hard springy grass. "Let's stay here. Why do we have to go on?"

He did not answer for a moment and she touched his shoe. Then he crouched down slowly beside her. "We're going on."

"Something did happen back at the hotel."

He rose and tugged at her hair. "No."

She got up. Though she did not believe him she did not distrust him. That was a step. "What did I miss," she said, "sleeping?"

"A glimpse of the Black Isle. A moor—very bleak, with electric pylons marching across it like a Roman legion—a dilapidated kind of moor until you come to a turn in the road and see Dornoch Firth. The Firth was shining, and all the little hills beyond it. I stopped and meant to wake you, but you were so faraway and innocent I hadn't the heart. I bumped you a bit at Bonar Bridge but still you didn't waken. Get in."

"I'd like to drive for a while."

130

"Later. I promise. Presently you'll see mountains in the distance covered with snow. We'll reach the mountains but never the snow."

It was a curving lane which Aidan took slowly as it wound along the side of the mountain. Above the lane the hillside was dense with trees while the wild river plunged below them through a little ravine until it broadened into the loch. They crossed a bridge into the village of Lairg, a gentle place of grey stone houses with yellow or red or green frames about the doors and windows.

She was smiling. This made him smile, and he said, "We'll have a bit of lunch but we won't linger."

The dining room in the pub was clean and very plain. The girl who waited table was also clean and plain and pleased to see them, bringing the day's menu, shepherd's pie, without consultation.

Halfway through the sweet, Maddy put down her napkin. "Perhaps we should go on," she said, her eyes suddenly large, her color paling.

"There's nothing to be afraid of."

"I know. . . ."

"Do you?" He held out his cup for more tea. When she did not answer for a moment he said, "Look at what you've already accomplished: one call from Edinburgh and you set the whole thing aboil. Your mother now has the embassy on fire."

"How do you know?"

"Through Burgess, the chap you saw. He's become a tiger!"

She asked sharply, "Did you talk to my mother?"

"Yes. Before I left London."

Her brown eyes flashed. "You should have told me."

"I should. I didn't." He finished his tea. "I'm very sorry. Your father is waiting for a call from Burgess before he flies here or stops at home." He looked at her with bold dark eyes. "It seemed as though you should trust me before I told you all these things."

She did not answer as she put her coat over her shoulders. Standing by the car, not looking at him, she said, "Tell me things. Please don't make me wait."

"I will if you'll not go off on your own, bringing my heart in my mouth." She did not answer. He glanced at her as he turned on the ignition. "Darling Madeline, you've been brave and tenacious. Don't change." He turned where the road markers said Tongue. "I promise to have no more secrets. To begin: I did see someone in the hotel at Inverness." His voice was casual but he glanced at her swiftly. "I saw a man who in London was pointed out to me as Claverton's personal assistant—unofficial, you know. He was coming out of the dining room in Inverness when I went to pay the bill."

"Did he see you?"

"No. I did not give him a chance."

"Was he after you or me?"

"Perhaps neither. Perhaps it was an enormous coincidence."

"It could be, couldn't it?"

"Oh, I believe in coincidences. It's hard to believe Claverton would take the deliberate risk of sending someone after you or me. And it's pure coincidence that I met you at Cloris's flat and am driving you now through a country blessed by heavenly dispensations. See here. I'm not going to talk about Claverton or his myrmidons. I'll simply point out to you that this is the only road to Tongue. It's a single lane with passing places. He can't take us by surprise. Now smile. What I liked most about you when we met was your liveliness. You were bright and intelligent though you were beginning to be anxious. I thought, this is a true girl. She won't let anyone down. Sit up straight. That's it. No, sit up straight. Do you want to drive? I'd rather you didn't because I'd like you to see the country. Up straight!"

She laughed suddenly. "No, I don't want to drive. Is this the country of the moon?"

"It's the land of my sires. Look at it closely. See how beautiful it is. How wild and full of wonder."

The moors, with sheep and wide-horned Highland cattle shaggy as dogs, would probably be haunting and desolate under the rain, but now the sun was shining. She watched and waited. They said nothing to each other but there was no anxiety in the silence. It was, in fact, a sort of understanding. Presently she felt as though she had come home. But what a strange home. She was at a loss to know what she meant. This land. The words that might have been useful had been exhausted in lesser contexts. It was the most solitary land she could imagine and yet not desolate. It was grand and living. Here and there one's fancy of hell was enforced but only because the land was so ungiving. Ungiving? An ethical word where ethics were irrelevant. This land needed no one. In fact there was no one, though the old milestones said that people had lived here once.

Around four o'clock they came down a steep hill and saw, across the treetops, the Atlantic and the North Sea making a conjunction as blue as the Mediterranean.

Tongue was a bright little village with gay paint on the houses, under the shadow of the mountains. Aidan stopped the car by a massive Victorian edifice with antlers over the door. "Where sportsmen came," he said, "in the days of the dear dead queen of my granny."

"Claverton's man—wouldn't he come to a place like this if he follows us?"

"Perhaps. Quite possibly. But even so, I think it's safe enough."

The entrance was dark, old-fashioned and empty save for glass cases of stuffed birds and a fox. Aidan rang the bell at the reception desk and an auburn-haired girl with a shining complexion appeared after a time, agreed with great

133

pleasure that "Aye," two rooms were available, that dinner was served at seven thirty, that it was a very fine day to be in Tongue. "On holiday?"

"Walking. With my sister."

Maddy followed him up the wide shallow stairs with the tokens of sportsmen and fishermen peering at them from the gloom of the walls. "I'm your sister?"

He did not turn around. "Yes. Welcome. Now which room?"

The first room was large and full of light. She went to the window. The sea reached as far as the horizon. On a spur of land a ruined tower kept a bold and lonely watch. "This room."

"Good. Sleep until dinner. They've very long twilights in the north. We'll walk about later." Though his hand was on the door, he came back into the room and kissed her on the top of the head. "Happy dreams."

She collapsed on the bed without taking off her shoes. Once she opened her eyes briefly to see the bright light on the ceiling, said "Ah, God" aloud as though making a prayer, and fell asleep instantly. She did not waken again until he shook her, and then she waked buoyant and free of apprehension.

Dinner had a touch of elegance, of wine waiter and *sole aux champignons*. She felt as happy as a jet of steam, with no relation to the past or the future. She argued and teased him with questions, then pranced away. She mocked him and then was serious while she ate her *bombe glacée*, but over the cheese she refused to take him seriously.

He did not mind. He did not need to put his virtues on anxious display. He told her once to shut up, but since this merely gave her more buoyancy he sat back to take control. She, for her part, was not bothered. No one had controlled her before, why now?

A black and white dog joined them when they set out to climb down the hill to the shore. It was still light enough to read a poem. "Read me a poem!" But he sang instead, a Gaelic song from his childhood and a Swahili song. They stood silently looking at the pewter water and pewter sky and at the pele tower on the spur of land, black in the twilight, its ancient power gone, now a part of sea and sky.

"What's a pele tower?"

"Our Scottish watchtower where we hid our wives and servants when the enemy came."

"This twilight—there's no end of day. I see why Richard wanted to come here. Was he very unhappy?"

"Yes."

"Would this have helped? Being here?"

"I think so. It's a country that's been terribly tried. It's survived with a measure of grace."

"Why was he so unhappy?"

Aidan did not answer for a time. He took his hand out of his pocket and ran it through his hair. He frowned and looked at her with cloudy eyes. "You get unhappy when you're not sure, when you've no base, when your faith is shaken. Perhaps everything had come too fast and too well. He wasn't certain what he wanted in life. It was backing up on him. I think he was frightened. He questioned his honesty—about the least thing, but questioned a bit dishonestly, I thought. It seemed to me he exhausted himself and yet avoided the questions that gave answers." He shrugged his shoulders and leaned back against the tree. "He began to believe in nemesis—and Claverton obliged."

"Cloris?"

"I never knew Cloris very well. I wasn't often in Zambia. When I dined with them I sometimes wondered why two such different people chose each other. It seemed to me something was wrong but Richard was loyal and it wasn't for me to ask. I'd made my own mistake." He hesitated and looked at her briefly. "I married when I was twenty-three and my wife left me after a year."

"Oh." And then, "Why?"

"Oh, bless you. One doesn't hear that question asked in such a wondering tone these days."

"Why?"

"It's over. That's it."

She blazed with questions but nodded when she saw in his expression that he would not bear any more. To change the subject, she said, "I think Cloris is in love with Claverton."

"My God, do you really think so?"

"She can hardly keep her hands from him."

"Well, that's a jolly show. He's got a wife." He whistled for a moment. "Perhaps he's more reckless than I think. Madeline—" She could not read very much in his eyes before he reached out and drew her to him, his arm across her shoulder. "I brought you here. I—I feel very responsible for you. Do you understand?"

"That you feel very responsible for me. Must you?"

He started to answer, then took his arm from her shoulder and turned away. He smiled faintly, and his eyes, very dark in the twilight, narrowed against the sheen of light on the sea.

"A surrogate brother—will you accept that until we get things straightened out?" His deep voice quickened. "All I ask is—let me be responsible for you until this is over."

So I'm in love with him, she told herself with no ornamentation. Irrevocably. It seemed natural and inevitable but saying it to him was not urgent. She put her cheek suddenly against his sleeve. "And me responsible for you."

He looked down at her. After a moment he said, "Fair enough."

"No independent action . . ."

"I think we make no promises but behave ourselves very intelligently."

She sighed. "You mustn't frustrate me either."

He agitated her hair. "Come along." Taking her hand, he

136

drew her after him up the long slope to the road. The dog came with them. "May I ask something?" he said diffidently. "Are you and that chap, Norman, in love?"

"No."

"Well, he is with you."

"No!"

"Yes."

She thought about this for a moment. "Not really. Only a little, maybe. We're just not strangers. We'd do things for each other." She glanced at him. "Do you understand?"

He groaned with a little self-mockery and put his hands in his pockets. "You're a new breed. I'll have to get used to your kind."

She asked shyly—and a touch slyly, "Will that be hard?"

"Perhaps not. But it's very different from good colonial conventions. I feel twice as old as you."

It was a silver twilight with deep shadows under the trees. Ewes and their lambs watched them, the lambs waiting with flickering ears for any unease from their mothers. The road was empty. Only a bicyclist passed, weaving stylishly back and forth to a whistled tune. The dog saw them safely onto the road and then trotted home. When they came to the hotel, Aidan paused by the car.

"Will that be your car?" a soft voice asked from the door of the hotel. "It's not locked."

"Oh." Aidan opened and closed the door. "So it's not, constable. Thank you."

"It's a nice little car—French would it be? Do you like it now?"

He was a solid young man with freckles, a short nose and a wide, heavy mouth.

They stood in the doorway for a moment. "It's not mine. It's rented but it's a jolly little beast."

The manager, at the reception desk, called out "Hah, Charley, stay awhile!"

The constable took off his cap to release a rush of black curls. "Aye now, just one minute of chat," he said, and glanced at Aidan and Maddy. "For if crime was to flourish this night, I'm thinking I'll be all places at once." He grinned at the manager. "There's no other law officer in the whole north of Scotland tonight but myself now." He laughed but looked briefly at the three.

"Well, what a state." The manager showed a red laugh in a brown beard.

"From where would you summon the full force of the law?" Aidan asked. "If you needed it?"

"Dornoch." The constable put out his cigarette abruptly. "Sixty miles the way the crow flies—but none of us are crows. There's not much to call out the law though, I should tell you. A few lads with too many glasses. And now and then a car in a ditch. And once in a time a man beats his wife or a wife beats her man." He pushed back his curly hair and put on his cap. "Though one never knows. The day may be close at hand."

"When P.C. MacQueen with uncommon courage met and mastered three desperados wanted by Interpol," the manager suggested with another great laugh behind his beard.

"Aye, that's what I tell the wife. Swift promotion and a good life for all the bairns. But she says, keep jogging on, Charley, never mind the rest. Well, I'll wish you all good night."

"Constable!" Aidan followed him out into the dark. "When do you go off duty?"

"Seven in the morning." The constable narrowed his eyes. "Why?"

"Where is your police station?"

"Bettyhill. Ten miles east. Why?"

Aidan made a sudden decision. He took out his wallet. "This is my card. I'd be glad if you'd remember my name. The young lady is the sister of my best friend. She may be

138

in danger. I'll look after her but—but I'd be glad if you'd remember my name."

P.C. MacQueen turned his electric torch onto the card. "Aidan Ross. That's a name around here." He turned the torch briefly toward Aidan. "Do you care to tell me more, Mr. Ross? Danger—now there's a word!"

Aidan hesitated. "No. If I say too much it will be my imagination. If we go west tomorrow where is the next constabulary?"

"Wester Ross—Ullapool. A long way, sir, down very delaying roads."

"Well, thank you, constable."

The constable turned his torch toward him again. "I hope you're in full accord with what you're doing, sir."

"I hope so too. Thank you very much. Good night."

Maddy had gone upstairs. He knocked. "Good night. Lock your door."

She flung it open. "Why?"

"Cold things walking up my back."

She examined the door. "There's no key."

"Damn."

"I'll put a chair. Are we really afraid?"

"Not really. Just a dry run."

The Seventh Day Morning

She came out of a very deep sleep into the light of day. It was morning. She realized that a soft steady rapping had wakened her, as at Inverness, and ran to the door.

"Maddy, can you hear me?"

The voice was very low but now she knew it well.

"Aidan . . ." She drew him in.

"Good girl. Claverton's man is here, and another man with him. I'll slip away because they'd recognize me. Here's my wallet and the car keys. You pay the bill and drive toward Durness. Immediately. I'll wait a quarter of a mile down the road."

"We can't run away! We've got to talk to them."

"There are two of them. I'll not even discuss it with you."

"Aidan—it's such a good chance!"

"Ah, you're such a bold girl! It's no chance at all. Madeline, I beg you! Will you do as I ask?"

"But what could they do to us here?"

"Know that they're on the right track. That's enough. I don't want them to have a clue."

"But if they ask, the manager will describe us."

"He'll not know which way we've gone if you're clever. For God's sake, stop arguing!"

She dressed quickly. "Oh, God," she thought aloud as she dragged a comb through her hair, "there aren't any mysteries that can't be revealed. Please! Keep me from being tricked by red herrings. Everything clear, clear, whatever happens next. Thank you."

Breakfast was being served and the smell came to her poignantly. The manager was presiding over the oatmeal and the reception desk was empty. She weighed the money down with the handbell. All desire to linger suddenly vanished. She ran down the steps, the key in her hand.

For a moment the car was unfamiliar but cars and she were friends. Though no one was visible, she started east to point any watcher in the wrong direction. When ten minutes later she passed the hotel again, going west, someone was standing by his car and glanced at her, but she told herself that the car, a grey Vauxhall, had been there yesterday before they arrived.

She repeated this to Aidan when he came aboard at the assigned place. He had been leaning against a stone wall, watching for her, his hands in his pockets, the sun very bright on his black hair and sun-browned face. Her heart leaped as he stood up smiling and made the classic gesture of the hitchhiker.

"Good girl," he said as he slammed the door. "Straight on for thirty-eight miles, and then if we're lucky some breakfast. Did you see anyone?"

"No. I drove east for a mile or so. But when I passed the hotel again, a man standing by a Vauxhall saw me. Was a grey Vauxhall parked outside the hotel last night?"

After a moment he said a short "No." She glanced at him. "Claverton's man came in a grey Vauxhall this morning," he added.

She reflected on this. "If he's never seen me—if all he

141

sees is a girl driving past, minding her own business—why should he be suspicious?"

"Why indeed?" he answered lightly.

"Problems multiply," she said with a good imitation of his lightness.

"To test our cleverness. Now I want you to pay attention to the most beautiful road in the world. I'll drive and you watch."

But she did not stop the car for another mile and then she did because he was right. Aidan put his hand on her shoulder. "It's said this is the oldest place in the world. These mountains began with time."

Abandoning the car, she went silently to the side of the road. The Kyle of Tongue, with water as blue as the sky, bit into the wild bleak moor which ran back to the mountains. "That mountain is Ben Loyal and over there is Ben Hope. They'll stay with us until the afternoon." Ben Loyal rose straight up from the flat land in snowy crags, Ben Hope as a white dome. They were storm and sun kings. Here one believed in nature more than in man.

Aidan stood behind her saying nothing. Finally he said, "This is where Richard wanted you to walk with him."

She frowned and wished to stay. He took her hand. "It will wait."

"They're strange, those mountains, aren't they?" he said after he got her back in the car. "Isolated, not a range. That look of ice on them is Archean gneiss, very rare. Now keep watching. This is land without recorded history. Only clan history, remembered from father to son, and now the sons are going."

She agreed the road above the sea lochs must be the most beautiful in the world. It almost made her forget why she was here. But after a time she said, "If that was Claverton's assistant, how did he know where to find me?"

Aidan maneuvered a bad patch in the road. "If Richard's

letters were in his pocket when he was picked up, I fancy they know exactly where Richard planned to take you. And when you disappeared, it might seem worth a few hours to follow their instincts."

"It was you started me up this way," she said with an effort.

He glanced at her swiftly. "So I did. I think the logic I followed is so simple they might follow it as well. In addition, because we must assume high stakes, they might believe Richard's schedule concealed something else." After a moment he said quietly, "I'd like us to agree on what we do if they catch up with us. If we can run for it—if there's any possibility of escape—we take it. But if there's not—and you see the countryside—then I beg you, don't struggle, don't speak, don't answer any questions—and most of all, don't let them think we know who they are. That could be very dangerous. If Claverton is so desperate that he sends one of his own assistants, we'll simply invite a firing squad if he thinks we'll identify him. Can you stay very cool?"

"Can you?"

"I'll do my best. There's a male protective instinct but I'll try to curb it. I think the fact that Claverton exposes himself to this extent means he's mad or immensely adroit. But then I can't read the minds of the powerful." After a moment he said calmly, "I must tell you you were on the B.B.C. missing persons' alarm this morning."

She did not reply immediately. Then in a small voice she said, "I must telephone and let them know where I am."

"Yes, but let's wait until midday. See what happens."

"What do you think will happen?"

He shrugged slightly and gave her a humorous look. "Think like them!"

"How will they think?" she persisted.

143

"Ah, dear heart! . . . Well, let me see. They want you —that's simple. What they mean to do with you depends on how they think they can use you."

"I have a key to that box."

"That's enough. If we can hold out till Ullapool we can talk to the police in Dornoch. The police can check our identification and get in touch with Scotland Yard."

The road wound through the inlets, and Ben Loyal and Ben Hope continued to rule the moors and the sea. On the road to Durness were only one or two villages of sandstone, though on a wild spur of land jutting into the sea they saw a bleak and beautiful stone schoolhouse and a handful of children in bright clothes kicking a football. Once Aidan paused and drove slowly backward. On this high place a little graveyard stood near the edge of the cliff, all the gravestones facing the sea.

"Aidan," she said, "will we come back here sometime?"

"What do you say?" he asked, not looking at her.

She shivered suddenly with shyness and longing, and did not know how to answer. She thought about the sea, not the road, not what was behind or ahead.

She discovered that bleak little crofts had been built to face the most spectacular views. Each time she thought of the Scots she loved them more. A broken croft, abandoned during the clearances, stood on a high knoll, and she turned instinctively to see what that crofter had chosen to face: a dazzling sheen of water and dark headlands. A crofter perhaps named Ross.

"After Durness," Aidan's voice was calm, "is Ross land."

"I'm not surprised," she answered. "Will we have something to eat in Durness?"

"Hungry?"

"Dinner was a long time ago," she said wistfully.

"Ah, lass!"

"You don't want to stop?"

144

"I don't want to lose time. I'm not afraid, mind you, but I'm reluctant. We'll have to stop in Durness for petrol and you can snatch some goodies from the post office shop at the same time."

"Do you think we're being followed?"

"I would be glad to know. I wish we had left a stronger scent toward the east." Abruptly he brought the car to a stop and scrambled up a cliff jutting from the road. Shielding his eyes with both hands, he studied the road from which they had come as it wound round the kyles. Then he slid down the cliff and drove out into the road so swiftly that she was flung against the seat.

"Sorry. There's a grey car on the kyle road. When I stop for the petrol, don't take more than a minute in the post office shop—don't wait for change."

"Is it—?"

"I saw a grey car. It may be everything or nothing. We're not taking chances. What's more, it is beginning to rain."

"Damn."

"I know these roads. Perhaps he doesn't."

At Durness, she ran across the road but all the loveliness of the village disappeared when she found the post office closed for lunch. When she ran back to the car, Aidan frowned. "You'll be all right?"

"Yes."

He turned swiftly into the road. "Good girl. There are no roads to turn off, and no short cuts. If we're chased, everything depends on how fast we can go. There's no question of hiding. A ruined croft wouldn't protect us. Abandon the car and escape into the moors? But as you can see, there are no hiding places. In about thirty miles we'll find a very chancy single-lane road down the mountain to the ferry across the loch at Kylestrome on the way to Ullapool. I'm telling you all this so you've time to sort out your thoughts." He smiled at her briefly. "And pray in whatever way you think best. Now, let us be calm and tell each other tales of ancient Scots. . . . Though, first turn on the radio. It's just gone time for the news. Find out if the police still want you."

For a moment static filled the car. She fiddled with the knob as the newsman's voice roared and died away, and rain mixed with snow began. As the flow of voice steadied the snow quickened.

"—of Exchequer expects no changes. Stiff questions are promised. The series of fires in Darlington are under control but police are not discounting arson. In New York, the United Nations Security Council has been called into session at the request of Zambia to consider charges of Rhodesian terror in the southeast provinces. The United Kingdom delegate, Lord Apsley, who is President this month, said at a press conference that his government welcomed the request and would cooperate in every way possible, as British responsibility for Rhodesia is in no way affected by the illegal breakaway. The session began an hour ago."

Aidan turned to Maddy and she studied him. "What does it mean?" she asked.

He raised his brows. "I don't know. The Zambians are cautious. They must have something. They don't believe in risks. Dear God, I wish I knew!"

The voice of the newsman asserted itself. "In Senegal, the trial of—" Maddy's hand reached out to turn off the radio.

"No, wait a moment."

"—floods in Italy. A special request has been made by Scotland Yard for any word about Miss Madeline Sayer, nineteen years old, an American citizen missing since Monday morning and wanted for purposes of identifying a body taken from the Thames and believed to be that of her brother, Richard."

The Seventh Day
Afternoon

Aidan did not attempt to slow the car but he put his arm around her and held her tightly as small screams built in her throat.

"Maddy," he said urgently, "it may not be true. We'll find out. It may not be true. For Christ's sake, be calm."

She was struggling to control herself, pressing her hands against her mouth.

"It may be a trick of the police. They may need you desperately and think this is the only way they can find you. Or maybe they do have a body which looks like Richard. Be—don't—Maddy!" He continued to hold her tightly though the road needed his full attention. "Oh, good lass, good lass. We must telephone as quickly as we can. If a call to London is too complicated, I'll get the Dornoch police."

"Where are we?" she whispered.

"In the middle of nowhere, my dearest, south of Durness."

They went another three miles before they saw a red telephone booth rising out of the snowy landscape. He

147

jammed on the brakes and dug all the change from his pocket.

"We're a sitting target here, even with this snow. Keep the engine going." As he put coins into the box he called out to her, "How far up the road can you see?"

She climbed onto a crumbling wall at the curve of the road, still struggling against her shock. "Hardly at all."

"If you do see a moving object, sing out and run for the car. These phones are hell. It may take ten minutes to get through." The cold struck at her face like needles.

"When I sing out you'll run too," she said.

The moors were as bare and mysterious as the moon. The slow flakes gave an illusion that took away time and space and increased her vision.

Watch. Watch. It became a metaphysical act. Watch and see.

Once she looked toward the red booth and saw Aidan beating his knuckles against the door and his forehead against the mouthpiece. She shivered in her thin jacket and stamped her feet. Down the road something suddenly stirred. She curved her hands around her eyes to focus her gaze and recognized a moving object. Aidan was speaking now into the instrument and she gestured sharply and scrambled into the car, putting it into gear. In the mirror she watched him running as though his leg pained him. In a moment he was beside her, slamming the door.

"A grey car?"

"Something moving. Did you get the police?"

"At Dornoch. They say we should head for Dornoch rather than Ullapool. The road is better though longer. At Laxford Bridge keep to the left. They'll send out a police car immediately but we're equally far from every place, no matter which direction we turn."

"Were they glad to hear from you?"

"They were glad to hear from *you*. And I raised a jolly

high fever about your safety. They're calling Scotland Yard."
After a moment he added, "I asked them to make sure that
a watch was put over that box in the bank."

She nodded. "Can you see behind us?"

He turned around to keep a watch, his arm against the
back of the seat. "Not a hope. Push as hard as you can.
I don't think you'll meet a car but blow the horn at curves
and that will give us a chance. It's about twelve miles to Laxford Bridge. Then, as I remember, it's a fairly straight road
along Loch Shin into Lairg. The police car should pick us
up before then. Maddy—are you all right?"

"The body in the river—what did they know?"

He held her tightly with his free arm. "Nothing."

The Assistant Commissioner for the C.I.D. at Scotland
Yard had borne three sharpening calls from the Home Office in the past eighteen hours because the Home Office
had been receiving sharp thrusts from the Foreign and
Commonwealth Office.

No one was demanding absolute clarity. A good deal
more could be resolved if nuances were cultivated among
principals while the police alone developed hard facts.

But the situation was mounting in tension, and when
Superintendent Patrick Fraser reached his office that morning, he found a message from his A.C. to come to see him
immediately.

Fraser was not only an immensely experienced police officer, he was also a politically sophisticated man with a
considerable knowledge of East Africa and Rhodesia, the
land of his birth, and the A.C. had the solid intention of
getting the best for his money when the best was at hand.

"It's sticky, Pat. All the submerged parts invite shipwreck.
The missing American chap seemed an inoffensive fellow
at first—working for a private American aid-to-developing-
countries program. Now we're getting electrical impulses

149

that something much bigger's involved. The embassy got worried when the man's mother called yesterday from Vermont, and last night the two senators from his state built up a fire with a perfect flap of cables. The embassy's steely grip has fastened on the F.C.O. The F.C.O. chief had me on the telephone three times last evening. The Home Office is also asking for full details." The A.C. was a grizzled chap, bearish, but very light on his feet both literally and metaphorically. Now he drew in his breath and blew out his lips and added after a moment, "The fact is none of them seem to know a bloody thing, yet something is always hinted."

"The chap found in the river?"

"I myself don't think it's Sayer. There's no positive identification yet, but I've got strong doubts. We've cabled the F.B.I. for identification out of the Civil Fingerprint File. They got his dabs when he got his job. It's the sister missing as well which has added to the funk. My instinct shifts the point of balance to Africa. You've dealt with such pigeons before. Get this cleaned up like a good chap. Yesterday if possible."

"Why Africa?"

"Information volunteered by the French Press Agency. It's about as cloudy as everything else but it has a ring of awful reality, and when you put all the known facts together they spell Rhodesia." He winced. "And the father and the mother of a row."

Fraser did not blink but he did make a small grimace. "If there are Rhodesian implications why haven't the F.C.O. chaps been unpicking the seams?"

"A block, I'd say—a most mystifying block. They're showing an almost catatonic reserve, but everyone suggests, in his own way, that some door over there is closed. They do this closed-door bit very well. You never even see a door. You simply hammer at a bare wall and manage to look a great fool." Now he groaned without pretense. "I'm trusting your massive discretion to move into those halls of power. You know Gerald Claverton, don't you? Sail in. Get aboard." He stared out of the window. "These quasi-diplomatic things are the devil. Many odds and ends will be cleared up when we begin to see their interrelation. Wentworth can go over them with you. Give me some kind of report around four this afternoon."

Chief Inspector Wentworth came to the Superintendent's office with his file. "The Lambeth division got into it early because Sayer's sister brought a wild tale of a tieclip. And her devoted boy friend badgered them for two days until they came up with an answer."

"Tieclip," Fraser read aloud. "Respondent Ted Eiseley located hiding out with girl friend Maureen O'Connell in Pincher rooming house, 4 Armstrong Road S. Maureen O'Connell, chambermaid at Chesterton Place Hotel, after persistent questioning, deposed that girl friend . . ."

Fraser closed the file. "Tell me about it. It'll go faster."

"It's not a very big story but it has its oddities." Wentworth scratched his nose for a moment and then searched in his pocket for a crumpled package of cigarettes.

"Eiseley isn't a skinhead; he's just a smart aleck. Likes things on the boil. Has his girl friend, a rather stupid little mick, polishing his shoes in more ways than one. But it took a lot of tough questioning. She broke first, which is what he was after. She says she found the tieclip in Room thirty-five at the Chesterton Place Hotel after the occupant checked out. She fancied it for boy friend Ted, and he fancied it, but being the sort of chap he is got her into a real snitter. *Didn't she know she should have turned it in to the management? Didn't she know she could be charged with stealing?* He just did it for kicks. When this Sayer girl showed up and positively identified it, the girl panicked and the boy friend—well, I'm no psychologist, and I don't want to over-egg this pudding, but I'd say he panicked too when he heard on the wireless that we were looking for Miss Sayer who had vanished. They don't think—fellows like him—they just react. Anyway, it was time for a few words with the hotel. What the manager said put our ears up. He said that Richard Sayer had reserved the room but never showed up. But Maureen deposed that she had talked with the man in Room thirty-five when she brought in towels. The description matched Miss Sayer's description. Maureen said he was an American, that he was taking his sister to Scotland in three days. The hotel flatly denied the room had been occupied on the night of May 10. It's true they have no registration. The girl Maureen got into an absolute spin when we took this back to her, wept and shouted that she was not lying."

"What do you think?"

"Well, oddly enough, I think she's telling the truth, though the hotel has the evidence. I don't know what the hotel is up to—it's a perfectly respectable place. Yet why should she have told all that stuff about Scotland unless someone had told her? It fits in exactly with what Miss Sayer told the QR Division about her brother's plans. And what young Norman Powell said. A girl who worked with Maureen at the hotel passed it on to Miss Sayer because the girl comes from Scotland. Everyone has the same story except the hotel." He looked at Fraser suddenly. "What about that?"

"Has the manager of the hotel ever been in trouble? Or any of the clerks?"

"We've got nothing. Manager's name is Whitehead, Colin Whitehead. His brother's personal assistant to Gerald Claverton, Permanent Under Secretary for—"

Fraser's low whistle intervened. Wentworth took off his spectacles and looked at Fraser.

"That's a thread you must continue to worry, but very

gently. Don't let go of it under any circumstances but don't let anyone know. Has there been any response to the A.P.B. on Madeline Sayer?"

"I checked just before I came in. Nothing yet."

"This young Norman Powell—do you think he's told everything he knows?"

Wentworth permitted a tight smile. "That kid is probably waiting downstairs now to add another comma to his statement. He is cooperating beyond our capacity to absorb."

When Constable MacQueen in Bettyhill went off duty, he had not been able to sleep. There was no logical reason for this. The bairns were in school. The wife was off at her Mum's. The chickens were fed.

Twice during the night he had ridden past the Tongue Hotel on his bicycle to take a look at the Renault, and he wrote down the registration number.

"Danger." The word had been used. Constable MacQueen was man enough to acknowledge that the word may have roused his sleeping hopes, but he did not really believe he was such a fool as to be trapped by such fancies.

On the second visit he paused to scrutinize the other car which had been parked outside the hotel before closing time and was still there. A grey Vauxhall with an English registration. Because he was a tidy man, he wrote down that number as well.

By two in the morning he was back at the Bettyhill station. He worked at a chess problem for an hour, made himself some tea, slept sitting up in a chair, and toward dawn took out Aidan's card and studied it. A man with a name as trustworthy in Scotland as "Aidan Ross" deserved respect. He made a written report and put the card in his wallet.

Before he went off duty in the morning he did an odd thing. It was that word "danger" which worked like a yeast.

He called the Tongue Hotel and asked to speak to Mr. Ross. Young Sheila, who answered indignantly after some minutes of ringing, came back to say pettishly that Mr. Ross wasn't in his room. "And he's not in the W.C. either. And for goodness sake, Charley MacQueen, we're not even giving breakfast yet."

"Never mind that—just take a look out of the front door and tell me if a wee Renault and a grey Vauxhall are still biding."

"Och!" She might be impatient, but she was his wife's cousin and in a moment she shouted, "They're still there. What should they be doing? Flying away like angel chariots?"

He said soothingly, "Just checking. Give a nice hug to the boy friend."

Now, five hours later, sipping a cup of tea at the kitchen table, he took out Aidan's card again and studied it. Studied both registration numbers. Wondered what in the world was going on inside his head. Stubbornness, his wife would have called it. Sheer Scot bee-in-the-bonnet, without rhyme or reason.

He climbed into his trews and his windcheater and took a small stroll to the police station.

The sergeant cried, "Charley boy! Has Meg thrown you out?"

He did not know exactly how to explain. But he did not lack courage and he made a clean breast. "It was that 'danger.' And she's a nice wee lass. And he is a Ross. And it seems if something's afoot perhaps I should not be sleeping, when all's said and done."

Sergeant Halliday took this without blinking. "Well now, there's nothing sinister come in—though there was a A.P.B. about a girl—wait now!—Madeline Sayer, aged nineteen, American citizen, height five foot, weight seven stone, blond hair, brown eyes—would that be right, Charley?"

Charley, listening with mounting excitement, merely nodded.

"I'm thinking that will be her." He was reaching for the telephone.

Across the desk, Sergeant Halliday could hear Sheila's voice. "Well, they're all gone—that Renault sneaked off like a poacher. No, no, they paid right enough, but not a soul to see them go. It's no good, Charley. I don't know any more. The Vauxhall? It went off right after breakfast. Half a minute now. The man—no, there were two—Englishmen —one was a bit vexed, I'd say, during breakfast—well, I wouldn't care to tell you his language but he was ticking off the other for a fare-thee-well. That's when they paid in a great rush and left, like I said."

"Give me the names of those two, Sheila."

All irritation had left. "What's going on, Charley?" she coaxed.

"That's to be seen. The names, please."

"We don't much bother about that you know, Charley. We just don't."

"No names," Charley said to Halliday. "Warn the hotel a bit on that. They're pretty slack. I tell you, we'd best be on to the Thurso men and the Ullapool. And a call to Dornoch."

Halliday was reaching for the phone, happiness in his eyes, a new grip to his hand. But when MacQueen said, "I'm thinking I'd best speak to them since it was I myself saw her," he surrendered the instrument with no ill will, recognizing the justice, and able to hear without effort.

Thurso had no word. Thurso too had noted the A.P.B., would be on the watch and wrote down the license numbers. Ullapool had noted the A.P.B., and the Ullapool sergeant's voice faded out for a moment as he engaged in a small colloquy. When he returned, the voice was loud. "There's something just come in! A driver's telephoned from a kiosk that a wrecked car's by the road—empty, he says —blocking the road, he says, he could scarce get by. Renault. Here's the registration number: NER S43H."

MacQueen's heart gave a lurch. He had to wait on himself for a moment.

"That'll be it," he said quietly. "Aye. That'll be the lass we're looking for. Get on to Dornoch straight off now, will you? I'll put in my report in five minutes. Empty you say. . . . That's *verra* bad."

Aidan had glanced at Maddy now and then to judge her staying power. Once he had put his hand on her shoulder and laughed softly. "May I link my future to a girl like you?" but most of the time he had kept his eyes on the road behind. The visibility had not improved, mist had taken the place of snow.

He had no complaints about Maddy's driving. She handled the one-lane road with perfect ease, driving carefully, for curves—as well as ewes crossing the road to be followed a moment later by their lambs—occurred without warning. When a solitary car came from the south she judged the distance between them so accurately that it was the other car which paused at the passing place while she continued without changing speed.

"It's about a quarter of an hour to the Laxford turn,' Aidan said.

"How soon should the police car reach us?"

"Not for three quarters of an hour, I'm afraid."

"You know," she said, "I don't think Claverton's assistant would be after us if Richard were dead."

"And someone very like Claverton's assistant is indisputably after us," Aidan said as calmly as possible, having glanced back. "He's directly behind us. Try to get beyond the passing place as fast as you can."

She glanced in the mirror and saw the grey car not twenty yards behind. With her foot on the accelerator the

Renault leaped forward, but it did not have the power of the grey Vauxhall. By the next passing place the momentum was matched; the Vauxhall moved into the empty space, swerved against the Renault, spun it sideways on the wet road and toppled it over.

Aidan, guessing that would happen, had time only to shut off the ignition and drag Maddy toward him. The car fell so that the driver's door was flat against the road. He forced his door which now opened onto the sky and climbed to the side of the car, lifting her beside him.

The Vauxhall was scarcely damaged. The driver had been so skillful that only his left fender was smashed; when the Renault fell he had swerved sharply up the bank and regained the road beyond.

Although there was no chance to run and no place to run to in this barren countryside, there was a reflex of defiance. As the driver of the Vauxhall ran up Aidan struck out with his foot, and the man dodged and lost his balance. But Maddy cried, "The other has a gun!" and that was the end of resistance. The man with the revolver stood a few feet away and gave directions.

"Come along." His voice was pleasant. "The more cooperation the less mishaps. David! They'll come, don't worry. This is all a jolly great flap about nothing. The questions are few and very simple—and none of this needed to happen. Okay, David. Of course, you understand *we* shan't be asking the questions so there'll be an interval of unpleasantness. And we must tie you up. Terribly sorry, but we can't trust you all the way to London."

David flung a knotted rope around Aidan from the rear and jerked it tightly. Aidan struggled sharply, trying to ease his arms, which were pinned against his sides, but the man with the gun said quietly, "If you make another move, Ross, Miss Sayer will be hurt. Around his ankles, David. Okay."

Maddy's calmness was not euphoric. She felt suddenly

157

an immense curiosity, not despair. After a moment she held out her wrists to David. "But don't tie my legs. I'm not going to run away." David jerked at the rope. She said in amazement, "I've seen you before! I rode in with you from the airport on the bus!"

He replied with an angry narrowed look. She flared, "You've tied him absurdly tight. Loosen that rope. He's not going to leave me."

The air was darkening for the mist was turning to rain.

The man with the gun waved it slightly with a faint smile. "He'd be very foolish to leave you. But we're not taking chances." As David tied her wrists the other pocketed the revolver and took a small knife from his pocket. "I'm really terribly sorry," he said as he slit the sleeve of her jacket above the elbow, "but it *is* a long journey to London."

She realized what he meant for David had taken a hypodermic syringe from his pocket. If she struggled they would control her in a more violent way. She looked at the man whom Aidan had called Claverton's assistant, and for a very brief moment she thought perhaps she saw him as no one else had ever seen him, a skeleton in love with death. She glanced at Aidan. All youth had fled, yet his eyes were blazing. She smiled at him, and he looked at her so vividly that her heart turned over. Putting up her bound hands she wiped the rain from her face.

"It's all right," she said. "It's all right . . . it's all right."

She watched as David pierced the top of the capsule and drew the liquid into the syringe. She winced from the needle and David's eyes flickered to her. After he withdrew the needle he saturated a square of bandage from a little bottle and dabbed the mark.

David had not spoken. He still did not speak as he turned to Aidan, whose jacket had also been slit by the tall, elegant, courteous and efficient colleague who now took her arm.

158

"You'll be quite comfortable in the back seat, Miss Sayer, and Mr. Ross will be there with you. We've no reason to stop till we reach London and the slight sedation will see you through. It all seems rather too bad, but the world is filled with quirks and oddities."

She slid into the back seat determined to sit up straight as long as she could. When the other back door was opened she realized Aidan's ankles had been untied for he moved under his own power. She leaned over and rubbed her cheek against his arm. "You all right? Your leg all right?" she asked softly.

"Darling Maddy . . ." His voice had become more natural.

The elegant thin man who had turned in the front seat to keep an eye on them said conversationally, "It's six hundred miles to London. No distance to an American. It will be a bit slow through the Western Highlands, but as soon as we get past Glencoe we pick up the good roads. And, of course, after Glasgow we have the splendid motorways where there's no speed limit. Now we won't talk. That sedation works quickly. I hope you're not too uncomfortable or too wet. We'll stop in an hour or so and untie your wrists."

He turned away. Maddy looked at Aidan and moved closer. He smiled down at her but, with his arms bound at his side, he could not move. She felt very drowsy. For a moment she opened her eyes wide and looked out at the countryside swept with rain.

At four fifteen that afternoon, Superintendent Fraser sat across from the Assistant Commissioner again.

"The Dornoch police had a call from Aidan Ross at one forty-five P.M." Fraser began. "He said Miss Sayer was with him and he was very anxious. Thought they were being followed. By a grey Vauxhall. Dornoch promised to send a police car to meet them at an agreed rendezvous but before the rendezvous could be effected the Ullapool constabulary reported a wreck; registration: NER S43H—the car Ross rented yesterday in Inverness. It appeared to have been neatly clipped off the road and turned over. No signs of injury—no blood, et cetera—and not a ghost of a passenger. That's all we know for the moment. However, a very tenacious constable in Tongue, to whom Mr. Ross had also spoken, took down the registration number of the grey Vauxhall toward which he too directed some canny suspicions."

The A.C. raised his eyebrows and Fraser shrugged.

"We checked. Registered in the name of David M. Dean, 35a Harcourt Mews, SW10. Mr. Dean is absent from London. He garages on the street. The car is not there. We have sent out the registration number and asked for an alert from the Scottish police. Any car coming south would have to pass through Inverness or Fort William. We're going on the assumption that the passengers in the wrecked car were picked up by the car which struck them. That car has made no report of an accident. We've checked doctors and hospitals in Wester Ross. No report of injuries. Aidan Ross, when he called the Dornoch police, seemed very anxious that a special watch be put on the deedbox of the missing Richard Sayer. We've done that. We're also watching Dean's flat."

"What about Ross? Who is he?"

"A Rhodesian. Third generation but with strong ties here. Educated in Salisbury and at Cambridge. His father exports sugar; very hard hit in the last five years. He's in the business with his father. He came up for some private talks at Commonwealth which are pretty ambiguous to me but seem to make sense to them. Our information all suggests he's not a breakaway supporter but is trying, in a rather roundabout fashion, to get some trade moving to the advantage of all. The F.C.O. people seem happy enough with him. His father fought Smith hard, but Ross's position—

160

no record." He shuffled his notes. "I've also just come from the French Press Agency. They're in a flap. Why? I think they're as bewildered as the rest of us. The London manager put me onto the Paris office, and this is the situation as far as they are willing to talk: their East African correspondent gave Richard Sayer *something*—no one seems to know what. He was to deliver it to the Agency's London office as soon as he arrived. He made an appointment and disappeared. The Agency's African representative showed up briefly in Paris, said he had dynamite which would blow up in their faces without the supportive evidence that Sayer held. That chap's gone to earth, they won't say where. Suggest he's getting a story in shape for the time when—if—"

"No hints?"

"Not a hint. But they say they'll be glad to disclose their wares, privately, immediately, as soon as they know what they are."

The A.C. took a long look at the river. "Tomorrow we'll have to get a warrant to open that deedbox."

"Good. The Agency chief in London—his name is Jacques Bernard—says that the Salisbury government has gotten into the act and is laying the groundwork for claiming this object—they call it a file—stolen, they say, by a foreign national, French or American; they can't seem to decide."

The A.C. kept his sandy eyebrows raised for a moment and his eyes unblinking.

"Fat chance, Bernard says."

The A.C. shifted in his chair, dusted his trouser legs, sighed and said, "Having cleared all the underbrush, let's get to what I must really know before I report to the Home Office: how far did your diplomacy take you with Claverton?"

Fraser frowned. "Nowhere." He ran his hand over his sleek blond hair. "He was tied up all afternoon with F.O. chaps. I verified this. His secretary was very ungiving, and

161

I don't blame her. I talked to someone else in the trade division but he said Claverton was my bird. I'll have another try. At his home, around seven."

The A.C. drummed with a pencil on the arm of his chair. "Not much to feed our masters. We got a fingerprint report from Washington. It's not Sayer fetched out of the river." He hitched himself closer to his desk and doodled on a pad. "Check me if I'm wrong but this looks a case we should back away from as far as we could—if we could. Confusion and obfuscation. Three missing people—though two of them have been heard from—and God knows, no policeman likes to deal with a missing person's case. Nine times out of ten it explodes in his face. No one knows what we're really looking for. No law has been broken that we can fasten to. About the only concrete fact we have is alarm—from a mother in America, from an embassy, from the F.C.O., from the press agency. What kind of evidence is accumulating? None—yet we can't ignore *none* any longer. Does anyone know the size of that deedbox?"

"No."

The A.C. reached for the telephone. "Get me the Middlesex Bank, Miss Barrie. The manager, please. Fraser, call me at seven thirty without fail—or as soon as you've left Claverton."

The Seventh Day
Evening

On a high rise just before the Vauxhall came into Invergarry, the thin elegant man (whose name was Oliver Whitehead) said, "Stop and we'll untie them now."

"You're a fool." David spoke for the first time. "You don't untie such people."

"Listen. A hundred things could go wrong. This whole enterprise is plugged with danger. I'm nursing a fragment of their good will just in case we need it. If we don't untie them their hands will be so swollen they'll be crippled by the time we get to the flat. How will that look?"

David stared at him. "You mean you're getting cold feet?"

"No. But I'll tell you one thing. Although he's immensely skillful, our master's being sucked in deeper and deeper and he doesn't like it. This could be very dangerous. I believe in some escape hatches."

David slowed the car and idled it by the side of the road. The rain had stopped but the clouds were still low and the diffused light cast a sheen over the loch.

He said unpleasantly, "I'm the one out front. This is my car. If any kind of alarm has gone out it'll be for this car, not for Claverton's Rolls. If I did this for you, Olly, you'd better be sure nothing happens."

Oliver extracted himself from the front seat and took out a penknife. He studied the unconscious Maddy, and worked loose the rope around her wrists. Her wrists fell apart on her lap. David, leaning his elbow on the back of the seat to watch, said snappishly, "Pretty, isn't she? What in hell does he want with her?"

Oliver did not answer. He lifted Aidan's eyelids. Satisfied that the drug was in full control, he cut the rope around his arms. Aidan's body sank slowly against the side of the car.

As Oliver closed the knife and slipped it into his pocket, he looked at the countryside. "Bloody desolate, but we'll come to a petrol station soon. Take on a full load. There's a bit of a short cut after Invergarry that will put us away from Fort William. Shall I spell you for a time?"

David shook his head. "After the stop for petrol . . ."

Fraser communed with himself on the best approach to Claverton. Fraser's uncle, a tobacco grower in Rhodesia, had married Claverton's eldest sister. This made any familial claims ambiguous enough to be manageable but left a sort of collateral ease. Fraser, however, was not certain how much ease was desirable.

He had a delicate maneuver to effect and had to be certain which atmosphere—office or home—would produce the best results. He smoothed his hair, examined his cuffs for any sign of the day's toil, straightened his tie and reached for the telephone.

Mrs. Claverton, he decided, would be a better bet than the secretary.

"Heloise, Patrick Fraser here. How are you? I hear you're just returned from a safari with Aunt Moll. Oh, rather! How is she? Oh, thank you so much. I'd like that. As a matter of fact, I'm trying to get on to Gerald. He's been tied up all day. Do you suppose if I popped in round about seven he'd spare me a moment—five moments, at the outside? Ah, many thanks. It'll be good to see you too."

He put down the phone and blew out his cheeks. Claverton was a cold fish, and Fraser had no special taste for ichthyology. Heloise was a kind, colorless woman and he wondered idly how she made out.

Promptly at seven he presented himself at the elegant flat in Hyde Park Gate. Mrs. Claverton, looking faintly flushed, pecked at his cheek. "Gerry came in terribly tired. He's lying down for a moment. I'd have put you off but I couldn't reach you. Never mind. If he's a bit short, that's the reason. This is a very good sherry. It'll cheer him up too."

The drawing room was very hot. The windows were closed and the damask blinds lowered. It was a beautiful room but peculiarly dead. Even the masses of pale flowers looked unreal, and when Claverton entered the unreality deepened.

He looked wretchedly tired, and with him, Fraser decided, fatigue took the form of a total withdrawal. He greeted Fraser pleasantly enough but he did not smile. Even his spectacles seemed misted so that one could not see his eyes clearly. He turned around a chair which stood at an ormolu desk and when he sat down managed to appear transient and tentative.

"I tried to speak to you earlier in the day—" Fraser began.

"My secretary told me."

"Nothing very devious. But we're reluctant to put questions below the highest level." Suddenly from behind the horn-rimmed spectacles Claverton's eyes seemed as sharp and dangerous as stalactites. All illusion had vanished. Fraser was so startled that he hesitated for a moment before he set forth his case. . . . A missing American, here from Zambia. His missing sister, who had apparently acquired as an escort (also missing) a Rhodesian engaged in talks at the Commonwealth Office. . . . Fraser made a well-bred

165

grimace and a gesture of apology. "Adds up to a sticky situation since the American Embassy is raising all kinds of high-level rows, and a powerful news agency is weighing in massively for purposes of its own." He added with an artful simplicity, "We badly need your help."

Claverton did not reply at once. He closed his eyes as though one more pressure would topple him over and when he opened his eyes again he did not look directly at Fraser. He turned slightly in his chair, crossed his knees and slowly expelled a breath.

"You know, Patrick, I'd do anything I can. I trust you. Moreover, it's my duty. But there's nothing I can tell you—nothing solid, that is. My deputy says he made this clear. Speculations, conjectures—but they're good only as far as they're sound. Ross—his father's well known in Rhodesia—came to England in an effort to find some sort of negotiable trade position. We've accepted the fact that he has a loose mandate from the Smith crowd but he doesn't show his hand. I've talked to him only once. Talks are conducted at a much lower level. You know this! My deputy offered to put you in touch. Why didn't you agree?"

"Because I'd already talked to the chap at the lower level and he said any directive had to come from you."

Claverton looked at him sharply and fumbled in his pocket for his cigarette case, which he eventually found on the desk beside him.

"That's idiotic. The whole Rhodesian situation is a mess and everyone seems to get his signals mixed!"

"I'd suggest you were the only one who can push the right button."

Claverton's lips closed like a safe. He flicked his lighter on and off and took some moments before he applied it to his cigarette. He drew a deep breath and expelled the smoke, then he rose from the chair. The cold eyes turned on Fraser fully before he spoke.

"I'll have to take this up with my superiors. I can't say a word. I'm as much in the dark as you."

"I don't believe him, sir," Fraser said, calling from a public booth. "I think he was badly shaken and was merely playing for time."

The Assistant Commissioner said, "Refresh me on Claverton. What's his position on Rhodesian separatism?"

"Some people will tell you he has a big stake in Rhodesia. Owns mines, has family connections. But they're my family connections as well and that doesn't mean anything sinister. I remember, in 1965, when we were all shaping up our Rhodesian relationships, he and my father had a bit of a row. If you had asked last week I would have said he had the traditional conservative attitude toward Rhodesia and you'd have to take that for better or worse. I'll do some specific checking and see what comes out. But I'm afraid this is moving into levels out of my class."

"Put someone outside Claverton's flat immediately."

"Very good. I've checked with my office and there's no report on a grey Vauxhall, registration number 21JB35, heading south."

"Ah, Pat, we can't have all the breaks. About that deedbox. It's a twelve by twelve. I don't know if that gets us any forrader. But I am convinced that it's got to have an iron protection. The bank manager has agreed. Get one of your best chaps over there before the bank opens in the morning. He's going to be put on as a teller and if anyone appears with the duplicate key, he'll be the chap they have to see."

"Good."

"One thing more. I had a chat with my opposite number in the F.C.O. He tells me that Rhodesia is putting in a formal claim through South Africa for property stolen by one Richard Sayer."

"Lumme. The Agency wasn't so wrong. They'll fight! But what?"

"As a legal maneuver it seems rather sad since Britain doesn't recognize any legal claims made by the Smith government. No attention will be paid. See me the first thing in the morning."

"I will."

"You said that wreck was found north of Ullapool? My God, that's almost on the Arctic Circle. You know, I think I'd be glad if you'd call me *anytime* during the night if you have word on those two."

When he closed the door after Fraser, Claverton did not speak to his wife. He seemed scarcely to notice her. He refused dinner and while she was eating at the large dining table in colorless dismay, he left the flat.

He did not know where to go. When a man sees his career falling about his ears and knows that he cannot blame anyone but himself—*unless* he can still pull it off—his range of vision narrows.

Too much arrogance, too much enjoyment of his own skill, too much commitment, too many mistakes by subordinates, too many signals mixed. He walked like an automaton toward his club, his thoughts as loud as words.

Yet he'd do it again. Rhodesia had been crucified. All the U.N. monkeys and the Labour party monkeys had to be taken off her back—autonomy and white rule, in or out of the Commonwealth, assured.

The anguish of the coded cables coming privately in the past ten days, the Security Council proceedings looming like a nightmare—they'd created a personal crisis into which he'd been sucked deeper and deeper in spite of his instincts, his training, his skill.

Oliver had not followed instructions. He had not telephoned a message to the club at six o'clock. Oliver had undertaken the dirty job voluntarily and Oliver was trusted.

Something had gone wrong.

The darkness of the streets seemed a greater protection from nemesis than his club, but he could not walk about forever. By nine o'clock he had given his hat and stick to the club attendant and ordered a double whiskey in the library. There, with the dark oak and heavy upholstery, he tried to engage his attention with the financial journals he never read. Presently he turned his chair so that no one could see him and closed his eyes. He forced himself to reflect on his future, as coldly and impersonally as possible. It was a dry and painful exercise but he did not flinch. Soon after the clock struck eleven, an attendant circled the library. "Telephone call for Mr. Claverton."

He sprang up, revealing himself.

Oliver sounded a long way off.

"Poor line, sir. Carlisle. I've two friends with me who'd like to breakfast with you in the morning. Is that convenient?"

"Why didn't you call me earlier, as I asked?"

"Impossible. Four?"

"In the morning?"

"Yes."

"Very well. Oliver—thank you."

"My pleasure."

The Eighth Day
Early Morning

David had picked up the new highway south of Glasgow and no speed limit had stood in his way for ninety miles. When the grey Vauxhall crossed the Scottish border and approached Carlisle, it was nearly eleven P.M.

"Swing into Carlisle for more petrol," Oliver had said. "If by some mad mischance an alarm is out for us, there's less chance the blokes in Carlisle have been roused than the ones on the motorway."

"Who's going to send out an alarm?"

"My dear boy, I don't know. But we did wreck a car, and we do have a pair of doped hostages in our rear seat, and perhaps a spirit of retribution saw it all."

"Jesus, what a bloody mess."

"I don't see that at all. We've been blindingly clever from start to finish. Caution's a part of our cleverness. Not to worry."

But David was sultry. He was an unpleasant young man when his temper was roused. Oliver made his call, bought hot coffee in containers, and sandwiches, and set out to woo him with jokes and badinage. He was not certain how well he succeeded; it took all the way to the Liverpool road signs to get a laugh, and after that he suggested that David have a sleep while he drove.

He was used to not sleeping. Driving in the night is always a mysterious experience. Form disappears, only impression is left. Decisions are made which cannot bear the light of day. Masters of strophe and metaphor make patterns for their lives which take no account of time or probabilities. Long ago Oliver had agreed to his own limitations; what happened in the night was carefully shielded from the day.

His connection with Claverton was personal and oblique. If trouble followed, he knew from experience that he would have to look out for himself.

But he did not really expect trouble.

An hour from London he wakened David. David responded quickly. He did not have to struggle for consciousness.

"What time is it?" he asked, trying to see his watch.

"Three. We've got past Northampton. That drug should be wearing off. Keep an eye on the back seat."

"Another little dose?"

"No. Strict orders they must be *compos mentis.* Perhaps we should tie them up lightly. We'll stop for a moment."

After they passed the Luton road signs, David said, "She's stirring."

Oliver glanced in the mirror. "Good morning, Miss Sayer. We'll be in London in less than an hour. Can you move about a bit?"

She did not reply but he saw her put up her freshly bound hands to rub her eyes and then lean toward Aidan.

"Is he coming around?" Oliver asked David.

It was another five or six minutes before David said, "There he is. . . ."

Maddy rubbed her chin against Aidan's arm and kissed

171

what she could—the raincoat at his shoulder. His face was dark with a beard, and the drug had given his eyes the opacity of fresh tar, but his voice was tender. "Darling Maddy . . ."

It was just going on four o'clock when they passed the Golder's Green Underground Station. This part of London was still asleep. Only one or two pedestrians and a handful of cars paid attention to the traffic lights. London was Oliver's city. He knew it far better than his soul. At four twenty they left Hyde Park, turned into South Kensington, and drew up into a street which had a sharp familiarity to the two in the back seat.

Aidan, still languid with the drug, swore. "Do you know where we are, Madeline?"

Maddy shivered involuntarily. "Cloris's flat."

"Yes."

Oliver took Maddy's arm and David took Aidan's. Maddy glanced up and down the silent street. Daylight was beginning to break. She saw Aidan look at the first floor, and her heart turned over, for the lights were on and if Richard were there—or not—she would have to be in control of herself. No mysteries, no mysteries . . . all very clear, for God's sake, please.

Oliver pressed the bell and the door was released. An unfamiliar figure stood at the top of the stairs and disappeared as they mounted, Maddy with Oliver's hand against her waist, Aidan with David on his heels.

She hesitated at the top of the stairs. Oliver took her arm and led her through the door of the flat.

She saw it as she had seen it the first time: the lamplight reflected on the beautiful plastered ceiling, and the white and gold curtains and the furniture, all in such immaculate taste.

Although she was exhausted from the drug, she also felt sharp and clear along a narrow band of light. The shadowy figure at the top of the stairs proved to be a stocky young man wearing handsome tweeds and hand-stitched shoes. He was speaking now over the telephone and as he put down the instrument he said curtly, "Coffee is ready and some sandwiches. Bring them in, David."

His voice was heavy; he carried weight in more ways than one. Glancing at their bound hands, he said to Oliver, "Get those things off."

Oliver released them and said, "Do sit down. Be comfortable. Oh, this is Wilfred Jarvis whom you haven't met."

No one really acknowledged the introduction. Maddy nodded slightly and Aidan looked at Jarvis briefly and sharply. Aidan's hands were clenched in his pockets. He moved slowly up and down, keenly tuned to sounds and movements. His hair was rumpled and once he made an effort to smooth it. The need for a shave gave a saturnine quality to his face. He had withdrawn into himself in a formidable manner.

Jarvis had gone into the bedroom. Raised voices spilled through the doors, his hobnailed, Cloris's—unmistakably Cloris's—shrieking a stream of words. He returned to the sitting room with the words pelting him, but he seemed unaffected and went to the window to glance out.

It was Oliver who stepped to the bedroom door and said lightly, "Come along. Have some coffee. There's nothing to be upset about. They've had a good rest and they're in good spirits. Come along."

Cloris's voice, close to hysteria, was shrill.

"I was promised—*I was promised*—this flat would only be used for messages or for Gerald. You've all lied to Gerald!"

Oliver said shortly, "Jarvis is in command here. That's the way Gerald wants it. Now come along and be sensible."

"I will not!"

Maddy's voice rose. "I couldn't bear to see her. Let her stay there."

An abrupt silence descended on the bedroom. Oliver withdrew slowly and closed the door. He said nothing, only took a sandwich and nibbled it absent-mindedly. He drew back a curtain at the window. "Oh!" he said abruptly, "here he is! David, go to the door."

Maddy sensed it was Claverton even before he appeared. At the low murmuration of voices on the stairs, Aidan came and stood behind her; her hand groped backward for his.

Claverton looked very tired. His fatigue and tension had been heightened to a kind of transparency by his vigil through the night. But he came in with great self-possession; his "good morning" had a certain lightness and charm. He nodded to Oliver, took off his horn-rimmed spectacles and wiped them with the handkerchief from his breast pocket, accepted a cup of coffee and sat down in one of the white and tangerine chairs as though the gathering were a small reception.

"Do sit down," he said to Maddy and Aidan. "This is no confrontation, although someone went to absurd lengths to induce your return to London."

The bedroom door opened quietly and Cloris stood behind Claverton, exceedingly pale, her fair hair rumpled but all the ringlets in place, her long-tunicked pants suit making her more slender than ever, her glance fixed so steadily on him that she paid no attention to anyone else.

His eyes flickered for a moment but he gave no other sign of her presence.

"Please sit down," he said more sharply, with a peremptory gesture. Maddy, holding Aidan's hand, moved to the Regency sofa.

"I've been put in an abominable situation," Claverton said. "A detestable one for a man in my position. I got involved when I tried to help your very foolhardy brother, Miss Sayer—and you have not made it easier for him or for me. Why did you run away? This whole wretched business could have been dispatched in three days if you had not behaved like a child. I assured you I had negotiating powers. Why did you believe this man instead of me?"

His icy glance, flicking at Aidan, was filled with contempt.

"Is my brother alive?"

Claverton looked at her sharply but did not reply.

"These three days have been crucial. We have now the extreme chance to carry it off safely—you and I."

Maddy felt Aidan's body stiffen. She tightened her grip on his hand until she felt him relax by a degree.

"I will not talk with you unless I know my brother is alive."

"Why do you think he is not alive?"

"A police report asked me to identify a body taken from the river."

"Ah!" Claverton studied her quietly for a moment. "I have absolutely no control over the disposition of your brother. My competence is very narrow. If you give me the key to the deedbox, and authority, I'm confident I can guarantee your brother's safe delivery alive by ten o'clock this morning."

"My brother must have a similar key. Why hasn't he given it to you? I'm sure you must have tried all kinds of ways to get it from him."

"I? I'm totally uninvolved. You must put such questions to Mr. Jarvis here. I detest the whole matter."

Maddy appeared very cool though her heart was pounding. "The key, without my authorization, wouldn't do you any good. I have no idea why he is protecting whatever's been put in the bank. But he's my brother and he's the only one I will take orders from." Her brown eyes were open very wide to prevent any weeping, and she looked from Claverton to Jarvis to keep herself occupied.

Claverton rose. "Then there is nothing more I can do. I have no control over Mr. Jarvis. I withdraw completely. I've

175

done my best." He turned slightly toward Cloris, a beautifully coordinated move. Jarvis went to the window and opened it.

With immense nervous animation Cloris said, "Gerald, you promised this flat would not be used—" He smiled suddenly and kissed her, shutting off her words. But the kiss seemed to stir her to a deeper agitation, something close to hysteria. "What is Jarvis doing! Jarvis, what are you doing?"

Maddy was also filled with a coil of tension. "Is he signaling?" she asked Aidan sharply.

Aidan put his arm around her. "I suspect they have Richard below in a car."

Cloris had surrendered to a frenzy of protest. She clung to Claverton but he relentlessly disengaged himself. Jarvis held her by the shoulders until Claverton got out of the room. Claverton's voice was raised with a shrillness no one had ever heard before as he went down the stairs. "Oliver, I don't want even a report on this. Nothing. Destroy everything in writing. Tell Jarvis."

Oliver's voice was calm, even a little jocular. "There's nothing in writing, sir. Nothing to worry about." Then he lifted his voice, calling David.

Maddy watched Cloris. Cloris had no more reality for her than a stick. Yet Cloris's anguish was so unmistakable that one would have to be a stick oneself not to feel some compassion.

Maddy got up and went to Cloris. "Why did you lend yourself to this?" she asked, putting her arm around her and taking her away from Jarvis into the bedroom. "It's *Richard* you're doing this to."

Cloris threw back her head as they heard a car draw away from the curb. She tried to control herself and pulled away from Maddy.

"Don't touch me!" She went into the bathroom and slammed the door.

Maddy stood for a moment alone. She knew suddenly that she needed all her courage. In an odd way, she needed all her innocence.

What if she did not know Richard? What if he had changed so much that he was a different man?

She stared at herself in the mirror, addressing the child-like figure with the rumpled hair and the flushed face. "What are you going to see? Make up your mind."

Aidan appeared in the glass, put his cheek against her hair and drew her toward the sitting room as he said, "Someone is coming up the stairs. You're not to be shocked."

He kept his hands on her waist. She stood behind a chair as though shielding herself. The sound of footsteps approached the open door. *What will I see?* she asked herself. Her whole heart answered *My brother.*

Two men came through the door. For an anguished moment, she fought to recognize Richard. He looked twenty years older—as though she would have to pass through a mirror of time in order to reach him.

She uttered a little gasp and Aidan's hands tightened. But she recovered. She ran and put her arms around Richard and lifted her face to kiss him.

He gave no sign of recognition. She felt as though she were embracing a tree. Putting her hands up to his face she felt it warm and lifelike but her touch brought no response. His body was there but what else?

"Richard. Richard. What can I do? Richard, here is Aidan. What can we do?"

She was straining to read his expression. At Aidan's name his eyes moved, but the expression of complete impassivity —or control—or withdrawal—or madness—did not change. The only faint interest he showed was in the room. He glanced about frowningly but nothing held his attention.

Oliver and David returned and stood near the door but he showed no recognition. When he saw Jarvis, who had not moved from the window, something seemed to leap in his eyes—or so Maddy fancied—but it passed so quickly it might have been an illusion.

He turned his head slightly toward the man who had come with him, a pale thin man of middle age, and the man said dryly to Maddy, "I don't think there's very much to be said. We realized you would want proof your brother was alive. That's all we're offering."

Jarvis spoke suddenly, with a tone of facetiousness. "The game's in your court, Miss Sayer. Do you want to keep it going?"

"There's only a very short time," the dry voice added.

Maddy said, "Twenty-four hours, forty-eight hours! What are you trying to say?"

Jarvis replied after a bare hesitation, "Look at him. . . ."

She did look at Richard; she could scarcely keep her eyes from him. She tried desperately to read behind the face, so remote and unfamiliar. But she sensed that even if great ambiguity lay in this facsimile of her brother, still the truth was eluding her. These men gave time limits for their own reasons.

"Richard—Dickon—tell me—"

Aidan put his hands on Richard's arms and shook him slightly.

"Richard, do you know that Zambia has brought charges in the Security Council? It's a desperate gamble because they still need the facts to support the charges. . . ."

Maddy, watching Richard as intently as Aidan was watching him—and as intently as the other two men—believed she saw something happen. The strange broken light in his eyes seemed to become whole for a moment, seemed to take on an immense life. But like a flare which illuminates with great power and then dies away, the expression faded and the passivity slowly and inexorably washed over him again.

Aidan spoke again sharply, "Richard!" A muscle quivered

in Richard's jaw. "Give just a hint. Do you want Maddy to hold out? She won't break. Do you want her to hold out? Just yes or no, whatever the consequences!"

Jarvis made a sharp move, knocking a chair away. "Damn fool—get him out!"

The middle-aged man took Richard's arm with a jerk. The muscle in Richard's jaw quivered again. Aidan held him tightly. Richard seemed to smile. It was merely an impression that his lips quivered.

"If it's not important—if it's not important—tell us, and we'll give it to them, and the whole bloody horror will be over. Richard—just a nod. Yes . . . No."

The illusion of a smile remained. He seemed for a second to resist the tugging at his arm, then he dropped his eyes and turned away.

Maddy fought against despair. She put her hands over her face, for she could not watch him go through the door.

"He's very heavily doped," Aidan said, his lips against her hair, "but I think he heard us. It's a kind of psychedelic dope. I should say he was fighting very hard, but he could not get across to us."

She turned weeping into his arms. "I don't care what he's protecting, Aidan. We can't leave him that way." She twisted away from him and said to Jarvis in a desperate rush of words, "I'll go with you to the bank."

Jarvis drew a deep breath, but all he said was, "It's seven o'clock now. You'll leave at eight thirty."

David loudly struck a match for a cigarette. Oliver got up from the discreetly concealed chair where he had been sitting and came over to smile down at Maddy.

"Good," he said warmly. "Would you like to rest for a while? Have some breakfast?"

She shook her head and turned away. She desperately held to an intuition: if she took the step of going to the bank, some power of civilized law would intervene.

She *had* to believe this. She felt around for the chair. Aidan sat on its arm and she held his hand tightly. She started to shiver and her teeth chattered, but she was determined to keep possession of herself. Jarvis went into the bedroom, and the murmur of voices—the hysterical decibels—could be heard again. David jingled coins in his pocket as he walked up and down the narrow end of the room. Oliver asked courteously if he could make buttered eggs for everyone but no one replied. After a slight bow he went into the kitchen to take care of himself.

Soon he brought a plate of eggs and sat down near Maddy.

"Where is your bank?" he asked.

"Chambers Street."

"Oh, yes. Well, traffic is rather heavy around there in the morning. We'd best order the taxi for eight o'clock." His manner gave a social cast to the exchange and she observed that he avoided Jarvis.

"Even with a drug he should have known us," Maddy whispered to Aidan.

"Perhaps he did. Communication's a very strange thing."

"Do I know Richard?" When she had asked this before, it had been rhetorical.

He pressed her cheek against his shoulder and said with great tenderness, "A wise question. You'll find out."

Closing her eyes against the roughness of his jacket, she watched Richard's face drift before her like smoke.

The sounds of day had begun in the street—car engines starting, doors slamming, children calling to each other, dogs barking. None of them, human, animal or mechanical, knew of Richard.

Once Aidan leaned down and kissed her. When she looked at him she saw how drawn he was; his calmness was a monumental self-control.

She did not intend to create trouble. She would get whatever was in the box and surrender it—but not until Richard was safe.

Abruptly she said to Oliver, who was spreading jam on his last bit of toast, "Whatever's in the bank box won't be turned over to you until Richard is safe with me."

Oliver coughed over the toast and blinked in the engaging way he had cultivated.

"Oh, I quite understand. We'll come straight to your brother—with whatever you've found in the bank. The exchange will be to everyone's satisfaction, and you and he can go off in the same taxi that brought you." He stood up and brushed his trousers. ". . . Into the fresh new day. After all, we're none of us criminals. Patriotism is still not penalized except by the enemy—and I'm sure none of us would use such a word as enemy amongst ourselves."

It was said so gently and charmingly that Maddy was, for a moment, puzzled. Then she started to answer hotly, but Aidan's grip on her hand became ferocious. The grip was so hard and unexpected that she looked at him and failed to answer Oliver.

Oliver took his tray into the kitchen, and David, who had been fiddling with the radio, shut it off and followed Oliver.

She put her cheek against Aidan's jacket.

"Will they give him up that easily?" she whispered.

"I don't see how they dare. He could identify them all."

"Then they'd have me as well as him, and the box!"

"I think you will have to use all your wits. I doubt if they'll let me go with you. I'll try to take care of Jarvis and warn the police."

Jarvis said, "It's a quarter before eight. Do you want to go to the bathroom or fix yourself up before the taxi comes?"

Maddy stood up slowly. Jarvis opened the bedroom door and spoke to Cloris.

"For God's sake," Aidan said to Maddy under his breath, "play along. Don't argue. Let them think you're as naïve as

181

you look. If you argue at this point they'll become savage."

Cloris was lying on the bed staring at the ceiling. Maddy glanced at her and Cloris's eyes flickered in her direction. In the bathroom with the door locked Maddy was suddenly afraid to be alone. Betrayal by the human animal still dismayed her.

She was now aghast at what she had agreed to do, and took as long as she dared to comb her hair, make up her eyes, coach herself in aphorisms of courage. Jarvis rattled the door.

"The taxi's here," he said. "Hurry up."

She looked again at herself in the mirror and tried to measure what she knew.

Cloris was standing by the bedroom window, her arms crossed and pressed in front of her. Maddy had the impression she was crying but now she had no compassion to spare for Cloris.

Oliver said briskly, "Ready? Got the deedbox key? Your bag? Good. Come along." He took her arm but she pulled back and turned to Aidan. "Oh, so sorry. He's not coming. Now do be reasonable. Why should we trust you? We need him as a hostage. You do see that." He took her arm in a vise. "It's a sorry business all round. But let's have it over with quickly. You realize neither of you would have a chance if you stirred up anything now."

Jarvis came up behind Aidan and pushed a small revolver into his ribs. "Sit down," he said.

Fraser was just on the point of getting his car out of the garage when his wife came to the front door and said he was wanted on the telephone. He ran.

"It's Detective Makepeace, sir. I'm calling from Drayton Gardens. Miss Sayer has just left with two men in a taxi for Chambers Street."

"Miss Sayer! Jolly good work! Can you watch the house as you're talking?"

"Yes, sir. I followed Mr. Claverton and that's how I found the flat. I think it belongs to a Mrs. Sayer."

"My God!"

"And there's a grey Vauxhall parked in the street, registration number 21JB35."

"*Very* good man! Has anyone else left the house?"

"No, sir, but this *is* the time people leave for work—"

"I know. You'll have to use your judgment. I'll get a police car over immediately to cover any emergency, and your relief as quickly as possible. I'll want a full report this morning."

He made sure a police car would be in Drayton Gardens within two minutes—he had a hunch that events were about to spring into the open and that a candid police car might not be inappropriate—and he made sure that arrangements at the bank were airtight. Then he called his A.C., who was still at breakfast.

The A.C. whistled. "*Mrs.* Sayer! It could be a coincidence."

"It could. A very sticky situation for us could also develop in the next half hour. If Miss Sayer does not cooperate with us at the bank there's nothing we can do. We can say we want to talk to her because she's on a missing person's alarm but we can't force a thing. We can ask if she's being coerced. We can ask if she is acting voluntarily but if she won't make any charges that's as far as we can go. If the two men with her are the ones who kidnapped her, then perhaps they're the ones who wrecked the car. If she denies the kidnapping, and they deny the wrecking, we haven't a leg to stand on, unless we contrive one very quickly."

"Our chap assigned to the bank—you trust his judgment?"

"I've every reason to trust it. We've discussed all the fine points. We've gone over details half a dozen times: Shall we challenge or not challenge? Shall she receive her deedbox in a private room or through the wicket surrounded by all the people in the bank? He recommends as many people as possible be involved. I think he's right. I'm on my way there now."

Maddy sat in the taxi between Oliver and David, refusing to be drawn into conversation, glancing out of the windows in order to maintain her contact with a familiar world. A policeman was on duty in the tangle of streets around Piccadilly Circus and she looked at him for a moment, putting her hopes in his hands. Oliver glanced at her as though reading her thoughts.

As they turned into Chambers Street, solid with traffic, Oliver looked at his watch. "Just gone nine. Very good. Now you know what you're to do? Banking is less formal in Britain than in the United States. It's a personal service for the convenience of clients. Where's your key? Let me see it. When you receive the deedbox, you'll open it, take out whatever's inside, hand it to me—I'm your solicitor—sign whatever receipt is required, and leave briskly."

She said softly but clearly, "I told you I will not give up anything until I have Richard."

He studied her briefly and replied with good temper, "Very well. Your solicitor will keep his hand on your arm. And if you make any trouble at all, it's your brother and Ross who'll be the losers. That's fair enough. David, pay the taxi."

She made a valiant effort to be calm. The sound of traffic roared in her ears, passers-by with faces and arms and legs but no reality moved between her and the bank. The passers-by were no more her friends than these two men. Her only friend was her dogged faith that law was more than rules and regulations and that somehow she would be able to reach through to that law.

Oliver's grip was painful. When she tried to loosen it he tightened his fingers.

Inside the door he asked directions of the attendant.

"Just round to the left, sir. It's clearly marked. The teller will take care of you."

The sound of their footsteps was lost in the carpeting. For a moment, when she glanced around, she confused David with Aidan and her heart turned over. Aidan might be able to defend himself, but Richard—the Richard she had seen a few hours ago—would not have a chance. What if this—whatever it was in the deedbox—was a death sentence for Richard? She stopped abruptly and tried to hold onto a wicket but Oliver was relentless.

What if I am killing my brother when I'm trying to save him? She gripped tighter and Oliver jerked at her.

"Behave," he said in an icy voice.

The appropriate window was well marked. The teller who stood with his back to them at a filing case turned around and said, "Good morning." Maddy opened her mouth to reply but it was Oliver who said, "Good morning. This is Miss Madeline Sayer. I am her solicitor. We wish access to her deedbox."

The teller gave a sharp up and down glance at them both through his rimless spectacles and said the bank preferred an appointment to be made.

Maddy felt something in the air. Her head lifted. "All right. When shall I—"

Oliver intervened. "That's a mere formality. This is an emergency. Identification is enough."

The teller's expression did not change. He was a man who had carried off several difficult assignments in banks, investment houses and insurance companies for his superiors at Scotland Yard. He agreed that identification was enough. He looked covertly and carefully at Maddy and the two men as he studied her passport and the receipt for the box.

"Got your key?"

She held it up.

He opened a small door in the rear of his cell and disappeared.

Maddy tried to separate herself from her companions in subtle ways though Oliver did not release his hold. She tried to quiet the awful beating of her heart. As they waited, a tall man with smooth fair hair joined their small queue.

The teller took longer than Oliver fancied and he struck the bell inside the wicket. The teller returned while the bell was still vibrating; putting a hand over it, he stilled the vibrations. The deedbox was laid just inside the wicket out of her reach.

"If you'll sign this, madam—and assure us you are not under coercion. Superintendent Fraser of Scotland Yard is directly behind you if you wish his assistance."

"Oh, yes—help me!" She wrenched herself around and broke Oliver's iron grip. "Help me! Help my brother!"

Oliver reacted with utter confusion and disorientation. He caught at Maddy, looked at the teller, at Fraser, in a series of sharp reflexes like a hunted man. But when Fraser put a hand on his shoulder and said, "You're under arrest for molesting this lady," he drew in a deep sigh, shuddered —and shrugged. It was David who ran—dodged past Fraser and darted like a football player. The detective behind the wicket blew a whistle, thrust the deedbox into a small safe and started through the door with handcuffs dangling.

Maddy said desperately, "David ran to get to a telephone!"

"The whistle was a signal to lock the doors and hold him."

Oliver moved his shoulders as though he disliked the touch of a human hand, and he frowned terribly as the detective snapped a handcuff on him. For a moment, he tried to speak and could not, and then he said in a parody of his light pleasant voice, "If David does *not* make a call by nine thirty, your brother and your friend will be in a very sad fix, Miss Sayer." He clenched his fingers and flexed his handcuffed wrist in disbelief. Suddenly with great resolution he recovered his tone and turned with a display of good sense to Fraser. "Miss Sayer's custodians did not really trust her and took some precautions."

"What precautions?"

"Oh . . . effective disappearance."

Maddy clutched Fraser's arm. "They're hostages, Richard and Aidan—oh, please, please, there's no time to waste!"

"Come in here." Fraser threw open the door of the private room where clients examined their deedboxes. "All of you. Where's the other one?" He peered into the corridor where a bank guard was pushing through a crowd of avid customers to deliver a stormy-eyed David. "In here. Lock the door." He went to the telephone and asked for an outside line.

"Ross is at the Sayer flat in Drayton Gardens," he said to Oliver as he dialed. "Where is Richard Sayer?"

Oliver gave a flicking glance at Maddy. "For all I know Ross may have been moved directly we left. . . ."

"We've had a police car watching since you left." Oliver's eyebrows rose, his pallor deepened. He leaned more heavily against the large mahogany table where his captor had stationed them. He glanced at David, whose face was flushed, whose eyes were moving angrily from one to another.

Fraser completed his dialing and gave instructions for the flat in Drayton Gardens. "Get that through to the police car and come back on the line." He did not raise his voice to Oliver but his eyes did not leave his face. "Where is Sayer?"

"Well, I'm rather afraid—" Oliver stroked his hair with his free hand. His dilemma was genuine. "I'm afraid you're too late. It's jolly bad. . . ."

Fraser, with the telephone in his hand, said, "You're a fool. Your master has too much at stake to protect you. You're expendable. I give you three seconds. Where's Sayer?"

Oliver blinked. "You don't understand. We're perfectly happy to cooperate with you—Mr. Dean and I—but that call was to come precisely at nine thirty and you see it's gone past that. I'm—I'm truly sorry."

"Where is Richard Sayer?"

187

"There isn't time. You couldn't get there in time!"

"Where is Sayer?"

It was David made an explosive sound. "St. John's Wood —58 St. Olave's Road. Flat 5."

". . . Get the address to the nearest police car. Have our chaps follow up with a warrant as fast as possible."

"Too late," Oliver murmured.

Maddy was as stiff as a tree but she managed to ask, "How long before we hear?"

"An eternity," Oliver murmured. His brow was wet.

Richard heard but he could not see. This was because the room had no light. He had lost all count of time. His senses were in disarray and he was willing to let them spiral and disintegrate if he could concentrate his will on keeping a narrow band of thought alive.

It was like straining with flabby muscles against a monstrous rock. Sometimes he thought he could never make it and that it would be easier for the whole damn avalanche to fall and put an end to this anguish.

At first, days ago, he had resisted the drug, walking up and down, up and down, until they had caught onto his maneuver and tied him to the bed. Then he had fought the drug by trying to recite aloud everything he knew—the multiplication table, the Lord's Prayer, the quantum theory, Abélard's last letter to Héloïse, parables and limericks, and he had—he knew—triumphed, because the drug which was meant to corrode his will and force him to answer questions had given him instead visions of great power and freedom. He talked incessantly about a million things but never what they wished to hear. By some instruction to that computer within him, the information they wanted was buried in a welter of inconsequence.

Now he lay very still, listening. The last dosage was wearing off. He congratulated himself on how well he had communicated with Maddy and Aidan. The shock of seeing them had shaken his balance, but he had spoken lucidly and clearly to them and they had taken over.

Listening he heard nothing. Perhaps he had been abandoned in the flat. Perhaps he was meant to get out and away.

He sat up and tried to rise. Blazing pain seized him and he sat with his head in his arms for a terrible moment. Then he tried again, got to his feet, took a few steps and fell with a crash.

The door was thrown open and light streamed over him.

"Idiot!" The middle-aged little man who had brought him to Cloris's flat during the night bent over him. "Rex, come here. Get him up. Was that the telephone?"

"No," said Rex, hoisting Richard, who was conscious and planning anew.

"Where the hell is that call? What time is it?" The little man consulted his watch by the light from the door. "It's just gone the time." He blew out his cheeks explosively and kicked at Richard in frustration more than in malice. "The whole damn thing is blowing up in our faces. Stupid bloody way to handle it from the start."

"What do you want to do—tip him out of the window?"

"Don't be an ass. Get him into the car. Everything okay here?" He smoothed the cover on the bed, raised the shades, swept a careful glance around a flat, impeccable and non-committal. "You're sure all the drawers are cleared out?"

"Luggage went five hours ago, dear heart." Rex's normal speech was sardonic.

"Walk him—that's right—you can walk, you bloody fool! Walk him right into the car. I'll be with you before you can say Jack."

Richard protested but the words were inaudible. When they got to the street he would run as he had run, over and over again in these last few days. His breathing was some-

189

what affected but he was not aware of this. He stumbled down the single flight of stairs but that was because he was disorienting Rex's equilibrium so successfully.

The daylight hurt his eyes. For a moment he hesitated. Rex wrenched at his arm and opened the car door. Richard stumbled again, preliminary to flight—free, disembodied, timeless—but Rex caught him a blow behind the ear and in a blaze of light and darkness he fell into the car.

The Eighth Day
Morning and Afternoon

The call did not come until nine fifty.

"Good work." Fraser rose as he spoke. "Where's Mr. Ross now? Good." He turned to Maddy and smiled. "Your brother is on the way to hospital. Mr. Ross is on his way to my office." She burst into tears. He put his arm briefly across her shoulder. "We've four people to remand. How do you want to charge these two extra fellows here?"

"I just want—I just want—"

Fraser was brisk. "It's all over. No need for tears. Mr. Dean, we're holding you for resisting arrest, Mr. Whitehead for molesting a lady. If you wish to call your solicitors, here's the telephone. I fancy Mr. Ross will have an additional charge to make."

Oliver lost his tone and his temper. His face looked like a skull. Without raising his voice he flooded the room with obscenities. It was again David who acted. He called a solicitor, spoke briefly, replaced the phone, and did not glance at Oliver.

Superintendent Fraser had a word with the bank manager, who had been hovering with discreet but explicable agitation outside the door, and took charge of the deedbox.

The procession through the bank was brisk and compact and accomplished in the remarkable silence that comes with a startling event. Tellers peered and clients, locked into the bank, stirred and stared.

On the street a small crowd had gathered. A policeman kept a path open to the police car and summoned a taxi for Maddy and Fraser.

"How soon can I see Richard?" she asked.

"This afternoon, I imagine. We'll telephone as soon as we get to my office."

"Where is Aidan?"

"By now in my office, I fancy." Then, with a glance at her, "Are you all right?"

Suddenly she felt as though life were a total blessing. She laughed a little because she could never put this into words. "Yes, I'm all right. A cup of tea perhaps . . ."

"Within fifteen minutes." Then Fraser looked at her and smiled. "I've only just begun to put together the pieces. You're quite a girl."

Aidan was standing at the window in Fraser's office. When they came in he said nothing, merely went to Maddy and took her in his arms.

Fraser put the deedbox on his desk, called the hospital to inquire for Richard and reported to his A.C.

"There it is," he said to Maddy, pushing the box forward with his finger.

She shuddered. "It belongs to Richard. It will blow up in our faces if we open it."

"I think it belongs to the French Press Agency, judging from their clamor. You have some charges to prefer, Mr. Ross, I hope."

"Assault and kidnapping."

"Good. I know Miss Sayer wants some tea. I've sent for it. We'll hear from the hospital within the hour. Will you use this time to dictate to the constable here your accounts of what happened, both of you? Fully. Please be comfortable. I'll just go and fill in my chief."

To dictate was both a relief and oddly extraneous. It told all and nothing of human woe and exigencies. What she had not known of his actions was now rectified, and the same could be said for him. Neither was long-winded; both were precise.

While the constable typed up his shorthand, they walked in the corridor, she in the curve of his arm. Through with wasting time she said, "I love you very much. Are we going to get married?"

"That is what I want."

"When?"

"Whenever you say."

She drew a deep breath. "Tomorrow?"

Fraser came down the corridor toward his office. "Mr. Sayer can't have any visitors until late this afternoon. He says the package belongs to the French Press Agency. He's adamant. I've spoken to Mr. Jacques Bernard there and he requested *us* to deliver it with suitable protection. It's gone. He also wants very much to speak to you, Miss Sayer. Will you call him?"

She nodded.

Bernard was avuncular, impatient and demanding. "Your brother's colleague is here in the office, the man for whom he went through all these high monkey tricks. He says you must be here at two thirty exactly this afternoon. Since your brother cannot be present, you must be his representative. You hear?"

"I'm going to be married tomorrow," she said.

"Well, what has that to do with two thirty this afternoon?"

"Nothing. I just thought I'd tell someone. Two thirty. The address? He'll be with me."

"So perhaps we'll have a celebration."

—————

After Maddy and Aidan signed their statements, in which Claverton's name appeared with no equivocations, Fraser asked to see his A.C. again, the statements in his hand.

The Assistant Commissioner was on the telephone; he gestured Fraser to a seat.

"We have no control whatever, John," he said into the telephone, "over the French Press Agency. I myself talked to the director but what could I say? We appeal to discretion and the Agency appeals to freedom of the press. No, they haven't given a hint. It's possible they have a story worth a million pounds or nothing at all. I strongly doubt it's nothing at all. This chap Bernard says they've invited a representative of the F.C.O. to show up at two thirty. Let me talk to Superintendent Fraser. I'll call you back in a quarter of an hour."

The A.C. replaced his telephone carefully, absent-mindedly straightened papers on his desk and leaned toward Fraser.

"Claverton. The Commissioner wants some deep and instant thinking before he talks again to our masters. Claverton must, by now, know what has happened. He's in his office but everyone's holding off."

Fraser handed him the signed statements without a word.

A deep silence attended the reading.

"Claverton must be mad," the A.C. said, blowing out his lips. "Let me see if the chief is still in his office."

He ascertained, sealed the envelope, gave it to his secretary to take to the seat of power. Fraser stood up.

"How in hell could professional civil servants let a thing like this happen?" the A.C. asked starkly.

Fraser laughed. "Ross guarantees that in Salisbury they're wringing their hands. I'm sure he's right. It's obvious something got completely out of control when some fool in Salisbury, convinced that Sayer had information enough to blow them up, confused himself with Henry II. 'Who will rid me of this wicked man!' Not having four knights or a C.I.A. he called up some poor sods who stumbled about doing monstrous things under our noses. All willing to take risks for an outrageous policy." He smoothed his hair and groaned a little. "I also agree with Ross that we will have a suffocating stink, a journalistic saturnalia and a very teetery government. And perhaps the end of Rhodesian separatism. But I'm convinced that no one in the F.C.O. knew what was going on, and this will be plain."

"Do you think the six sacrificial goats will go quietly?"

Fraser shrugged.

"What kind of evidence do we have that will stand up to a clever lawyer?" the A.C. asked.

"That's our weakest point."

The A.C. stopped diddling at his desk and lifted his eyes to Fraser. "What will Claverton do?"

Claverton was perfectly calm. The worst had happened. It was all over. An extremely discreet call had come as he talked to a distinguished visitor from India and he had not moved a muscle nor had a shadow fallen over the charm he was expending.

It was now eleven thirty, and he had not been alone for a moment to think or to plan. A blazing headache was appearing over the horizon of his mind. He could only afford the headache if it permitted him to go home and receive no calls. But he did not really believe that would help very much.

Everyone had been picked up and remanded, though not of course his secretary, the admirable Miss Sarah Watts, who knew a bit but not much and could be trusted in any case to be the goddess of discretion.

For a moment he lost the train of conversation with his visitor as he wondered if there would be any discretion among the six arrested. Six had been too many. He was a fool not to have hesitated.

To his visitor, he excused his lapse of attention by referring to a beastly headache. This gave him a moment's peace as he asked Miss Watts to fetch him an aspirin and a glass of water.

The Rhodesian desk two floors removed from Claverton received a call from the deputy Permanent Under Secretary. It was an uneasy, clipped and abstracted call, appropriate between two government priests who were moving through a thicket of appalling conjecture and unsteady facts.

"The missing Richard Sayer has been found."

"Thank God. Intact?"

"In hospital for the moment. But with a story to unfold. An odd bag of well-bred colonials have been picked up by the police, and I'm very much afraid the ball is now in your court, my dear fellow, and the very good health of our team depends on how you play it."

The Rhodesian desk was silent for a moment. "I can't believe it. Claverton is such a good chap. Went to school with my brother. . . ."

A sigh traveled from the deputy Permanent Under Secretary. "The French Press Agency has asked for a representative to be present in their office at two thirty. Would you care to assign a noncommittal sort of chap?"

The Rhodesian desk hesitated. "Done."

Maddy and Aidan had walked relentlessly since they left Scotland Yard. She had not wanted to return to her hotel at all—or at least not until all the answers were available. He had not wanted to go to his flat for the same reason—entangling ambiguities had first to be done with.

They were both sensible and sensitive but their hands clung together and, if separated for a moment, sought each other again.

"Why do you love me?" she asked suddenly.

"You're a girl with passionate loyalty but your eyes stay open. Why do you love me?"

"You always make people give a good showing of themselves."

"Oh, Maddy! I love you for many reasons."

"I expect so. Just as I do. I'd better call Norman."

"Why?"

"I think he made the police listen to you and that got everything going right up to this moment. Anyway, he has a right to know."

"Here's a kiosk. Have you enough change?"

When she finished the call there was color in her cheeks. "It's beginning to seem more real," she said. "We're going to have dinner with Norman and George and Sandra."

"Darling, they're your bridal party, not mine. I suspect Richard will have some cables to send off, and I rather fancy I'll be tied up this evening with the F.C.O. people. They'll need to lay some very respectable plots and counterplots in order to minimize the effects of Claverton."

"Will this be our world in the future?"

"Perhaps."

"In Rhodesia?"

"I don't know. Do you mind?"

"No. Just don't leave me out."

At two fifteen they took a taxi. He had not limped at all while they were walking. "Are you curious, my darling?" he asked. "This damned mystery has been your life for over a week."

She did not answer for a moment. Then she said, "I'm terrified."

The French Press Agency office was small, modern and, at the moment, vibrant with a private excitement. Bernard met her with a forceful greeting and a kiss on both cheeks.

He welcomed Aidan with a click of the heels and formal congratulations.

Sweeping forward a slim young man with bright eyes, a perpetual half-smile and a burning cigarette between his fingers, Bernard said, "Here is your brother's colleague, the author of all your misfortunes, Raoul Dubas. Allow me also to present Madame Mwiinga, the Zambian High Commissioner, Mr. Hilary Bragg of the Foreign and Commonwealth Office and Mr. Sven Johannsen, the United Nations representative in London. You are our guests. I ask you to be seated in here. Very good. The deposition of what we are about to show you concerns the French Press Agency alone, but I think the action we must take will be spontaneously agreeable to all. Now you see the contents of that package so closely protected by Mr. Richard Sayer, a veritable hero, is a reel of film. We will show you the film, and then you will ask Mr. Dubas any questions you choose. Our account of this *coup de cinéma* is appearing in tomorrow's *Le Matin*. You are comfortable? *Voilà*. Lights off."

The whirr of the projector and the light appearing on the screen had the element of unreality that always accompanies apprehension or anticipation. At first Maddy was confused. The film seemed to start in the midst of a broken action. An African woman was flinging up her arms and running, another woman was seizing a child and running. With the rattle of machine-gun fire all three fell, though the child struggled to his feet until half his head was blown off.

Aidan drew in his breath and expelled it on a slow flow of curses. The Zambian High Commissioner said in a clear sweet voice, "This is it! This is it! Oh, my God, where's the telephone?"

Bernard's voice in the dark was commanding, "Madame, wait. It is only ten minutes. You must pay strict attention."

Maddy prayed to have her attention pulled from the screen but she continued to watch. Aidan drew her arm through his and she felt the muscles of his arm tighten till they were like stone. The massacre went on, a horror of such proportion that the mechanical intermediary of the film projector vanished. The cries, the bullets tearing into the black bodies, the hoarse shouts of the police, the sweat, the stench of fear, the agony and the insane slaughter were here in this room. Occasionally the image was blurred as though the man holding the camera had lost his balance. But recovery was swift, and the relentless recording of death went on, now and then obscured by trees as the photographer made for another vantage point.

Village huts were set afire, and when the women and children ran out they were shot down.

Men, tied together, were driven to the edge of a gully and machine-gunned into their graves. A wounded dog creeping into the bush was caught by a bullet and jerked into the air.

The United Nations representative's voice rang out. "It is imperative that I speak to New York!" He and the Zambian High Commissioner rose so quickly that their chairs were knocked over.

"Wait!" Bernard commanded. "One moment more."

As the reel ran out a young policeman turned toward the camera, and in his eyes and open mouth and raised arm was the frenzy and despair of a man who had lost all contact with life, with himself, with coherence.

"This is when I ran." Dubas's voice came out of the darkness as clear and normal as the electric lights which were now switched on. "That man was the only one who realized what I was doing and his attention was diverted a moment later." Then he added gently and sorrowfully, "It was to have been the ordinary arrest of a man who had escaped from detention. But some of the man's people laid

199

an ambush. A policeman was wounded and the rest went crazy." He sounded almost apologetic, and relit his cigarette as though he had talked too much.

"Questions, mesdames, messieurs?" Bernard asked.

Maddy had hidden her face against Aidan's shoulder. He held her hand so tightly that she thought he would break a bone. She glanced at him and his face was white, sweat on his forehead. She fumbled for a handkerchief and wiped his face and for a moment he held her hand against his cheek.

"Its authenticity?" asked Hilary Bragg, moving abruptly in his chair.

Aidan answered hoarsely as though against his will. "Not to be doubted."

Bernard said, "Our integrity is behind its authenticity."

Dubas said, "Its provenance is this: I asked to accompany any police patrol that might be sent on a routine check of a trouble spot. I was, of course, refused. Then signals were mixed. I got word late at night that a patrol was starting at dawn for a routine display of authority and I was attached to it. How? One doesn't ask questions. I had my camera, a Bolex, and a tape recorder. Both are small and no one noticed. Everyone said the whole thing was routine but you see it was not routine. I started to take pictures as soon as possible. When I realized what I had, and the danger, I found my jeep and got away. I spent the night developing it, and then I knew I had a hot potato. I will tell you I was scared—not for myself but afraid I would somehow be tricked out of it. I could myself have eft by the first plane in the morning, but I wanted to follow up on the story—see what would happen, how the government would handle it, what word might leak out. I telephoned my friend Richard Sayer who I knew was in Salisbury. I asked him to come to my flat. He came at six in the morning. He's a friend of Mutti, though I never asked his political feeling. I ran off the film and told him it might be lost if he didn't help. He said he would take it with him that day to Lusaka and on to London if he heard nothing from me. I was left free for a few hours, and then I was told I could not leave the country nor use the telephone. No one gave a reason. I could not deny I was with the patrol because no one asked me. The government apparently did not wish to acknowledge the possibility of the film. My apartment was ransacked. Also my office. How they got on to Richard Sayer, I don't know. Perhaps he made an indiscreet call. That's all I can imagine. Finally they let me go—to make matters no worse than they were, perhaps, after the London debacle."

The United Nations representative had located the telephone. He put in his call, and while he was waiting, the Zambian High Commissioner called her embassy to dictate a report to Lusaka. Maddy's face was still buried against Aidan's shoulder. Dubas sat on his heels in front of them. "When may I see Richard? We wish the London end of my story." Aidan did not answer for a moment and seemed to find it hard to speak. Then he frowned and half smiled and said wryly, "That's putting your foot into diplomacy. Are you prepared?"

Dubas's bright, half-smiling expression did not change. He waited with alertness and discretion. Aidan drew in his breath deeply and shook his head as though he too had to start completely afresh.

"I'm a Rhodesian," he said unblinkingly, as though light and dark, mystery and pragmatism, truth and error must somehow be separate. Dubas nodded, his eyes attentive. "Salisbury will deny its authenticity but it will be their word against a good many others. This could mean the end of separatism."

"Richard Sayer—when will I see him?" Dubas prompted.

"Ask the doctor. But I'll tell you one thing: I don't believe Richard will say a word until he knows what has happened to Mutti."

Dubas stood up. The smoke from his cigarette obscured his face for a moment. "I'll get on the telephone immediately and try to find out."

The F.C.O. representative had a word with them also, sitting in the chair next to Maddy.

"Mr. Ross, Miss Sayer, if you would be kind enough to come now to my office and have a confidential word about your contact with Mr. Claverton you will be assisting in a most felicitous way."

"We are going to my brother in the hospital," Maddy said, leaning back against Aidan.

"I understand. But I fancy your brother would prefer to have this cleared up as quickly as possible. . . ."

Aidan said shortly, "Let's find a private office here for ten minutes. And I will be at your disposal for the evening, sir."

Bragg nodded, rose, rubbed his closely shaved face with his knuckles and looked about for Bernard.

As they went to Bernard's office, Aidan said to Bragg with an irony that somehow managed to be pleasant, "Has Claverton left on holiday yet? Will he resign over the weekend or will he be left to manage as best he can till all the evidence is in? Or will the F.C.O. face up manfully to Rhodesian policy?"

Hilary Bragg's smile was chilly but his manner showed he was nobody's fool. "The more you tell us, the more intelligently we will be able to conduct ourselves."

The Eighth Day
Evening

It was five o'clock before they came into Richard's room. Richard was sitting up, his thick hair brushed to a russet smoothness, a look of exhaustion around the hollows of his face and in his eyes. His manner, however, was controlled.

After the faintest hesitation, as though reassuring himself, he held out his arms to Maddy. She ran to him and huddled on the bed beside him. He held her closely and looked at Aidan with an odd hooded glance and only after a moment held out his free hand. Nothing was said. A shadow passed over Richard's face and then he made a visible effort. He pulled himself higher in the bed, forcing Maddy also to sit up, drew in a deep breath and gave a kind of frowning smile.

"Don't lean against me. That's it. Do I look all right?" He waited, his eyes on Aidan.

Aidan answered, "Yes. A new Richard, perhaps, but in the same line."

"Do I look all right?" he asked Maddy, glancing at her briefly, his words faltering somewhat as though there was still a poor connection between thought and speech.

"Yes."

He leaned back against the pillows. "I can't think very long in a straight line . . . but I'm beginning to stay together. Do you need to ask questions?"

"Our chaps have to know as much as they can," Aidan said gently. Richard nodded slightly. "Do you remember what you told the Claverton crowd?"

Richard closed his eyes. "I'd swear nothing. That's why they loosened me up with this damn junk. I seemed to stay together in the center . . . though maybe I went to pieces around the edges."

"Sometimes it makes you think you've been discreet when you've talked your head off."

Richard did not reply for so long that it seemed as though he had turned himself off. At length with an exhausted passion he whispered, "But they didn't win. . . ."

"No."

His eyes were closed. "I've still got another fellow sitting on my shoulder. There are two of us. Those drugs tell you what you'd like to believe. Yet, you know, when I wasn't doped I found something—that all I wanted was my integrity. I got it back. Didn't I?"

"Had you lost it?" Aidan asked.

Richard was silent for a long time, and then he drew Maddy back against him. "Well, maybe no—but I'd lost the answers."

Aidan said, "Tell us what you can."

Richard half closed his eyes and spoke very carefully, as though afraid of being jarred by the vibration of words. "At first they just kept asking questions. Tried to get that bank key. I didn't have it. I had mailed it to myself at a post office address. I don't think they knew what I had. I'm not sure. They kept speaking of the file but I don't think they knew what they wanted. They told me they had Mutti. That was when they used the word *film* and gave me a

204

shock. But then right after they said, 'You have the file but we have Mutti. It's up to you what happens to him.'" Richard shook his head and continued to shake it as though the action were involuntary. "I didn't know the truth about anything—whether Dubas had talked, whether the massacre was common knowledge." His face was washed with exhaustion. Maddy whispered, "There's plenty of time to talk about this later."

But he drove his teeth into his lip and shook his head. "All those fellows—Jarvis and the others—they're the kind of fellows you have dinner with—and marry their sisters . . . Jarvis—he's as good as a friend until he starts going on and on about keeping the blacks down and dying for Smith. Then he's insane." He looked at Aidan as though on the verge of tears. "They're countrymen of *yours*. How can they be murderers?" He began to laugh against Maddy's shoulder. She held him tightly.

Aidan asked quietly, "What about Claverton?"

"I couldn't make head or tail of him. I only saw him once, very disconnected. He said he could negotiate for me if my sister cooperated. He knew she had a key to the deedbox."

"Did you believe him?"

"I didn't believe anyone! I was going to pieces!" He began to weep, the tears going unnoticed down his cheeks. "But I hung on to the conviction that if I protected the film the political climate back there might change. That held me together. Then I thought 'But if I'm stubborn I can cause the death of my friend,' and that unraveled me again."

"Did you know the pressure they were putting on Maddy?"

Again he took a long time to answer, lying back, his eyes closed, the lashes damp on his cheeks. His voice was drifting. "I didn't really know where she was—they might be lying. Before they started on the drug I took some calculated risks. Maddy was one of those risks. I tried to think what she'd do when I didn't show up. She might go off on her own. She might return home immediately. I hadn't a clue. We're a terribly independent family. I had to act in the dark. I had to separate what they told me from my instinct to distrust them. A real risk because they might have been telling the truth." He opened his eyes wide. "Know the truth? How? How do you know it?" He groaned and half drifted again. "I had to hope also that Maddy was alarmed and doing something. I didn't have a single certain fact."

His face was white and he seemed to sleep for a moment. Maddy rubbed his hands. He opened his eyes and looked straight at her. "Yet for all I knew you might be five jumps ahead of them all the time."

She continued to rub his hands. "Are you cold?"

He shook his head and made a small sound like laughter. "But toward the end . . . you and Mutti . . . became more important than . . . But I didn't have the key!" He raised himself and spoke to Aidan. "Have you talked with any of Mutti's people?"

"Nabuku, here in London." Aidan added ironically, "They made a tough choice. They decided that whatever you had must be more important than a single man. They were willing to sacrifice Mutti."

Richard groaned. "Where is Mutti?"

"We'll know very soon. We think—with all this breaking open publicly—he's all right. A copy of the film is going to the United Nations tonight. Much more important, the Zambian High Commissioner has persuaded the Press Agency to have a high-level press conference here, in London, tomorrow noon, show the film and present the supportive evidence."

Richard sank back and closed his eyes. "That will do it.

Thank God. That will blow the lid. You don't need anything else." He opened his eyes. "You'll be there?"

Aidan looked at Maddy. She said, "We're getting married at noon." Richard studied them, one after the other. "That makes sense. . . ."

Aidan rose. "Good sense. Tell me, how, in God's name, did you let yourself be picked up in London—in full daylight?"

Richard made a mocking sound. "Do ask. When I got off the plane in London, a fellow I knew from Salisbury was hanging around. He said he had just gotten in. He offered to drive me to London—he insisted on driving me to London. That's when the warning voices began. I knew my plane was the only one that had just gotten in from Africa. That film was burning a hole in my briefcase. I had a hell of a time getting rid of him. I called the French Press Agency from the airport and found Bernard would not be back from Paris until the next morning at ten. I suppose I should have just left the film at the Agency but the longer I had it the more responsible I felt. I went to the bank and then sent Maddy a cable."

"But still you got picked up. How could it happen?"

"Oh, they never got off my tail. And they told me they followed Maddy from the moment she left the plane. I was so uneasy I registered at the hotel under a name that I hoped would be a code for Maddy if I wasn't able to meet her at the airport. I called Bernard's office again to make sure he was expected. I was going to insist he go with me to the bank to collect the film. Then I fell for the oldest trick of all, someone you trust. In the hotel, when I came down to go out, I ran into a good fellow I knew, a good reliable trustworthy son of a bitch. I would *almost* have trusted him with the film if I had had it. Almost. I suppose he was one of those trailing me. We were terribly glad to see each other. I think the hotel put him onto me. I don't know how. He offered to drive me wherever I was going. I was still cunning enough to say Berkeley Square, not Bond Street. We picked up Jarvis, whom I didn't know, at the Dorchester. And it was Jarvis who banged me on the back of the head." He mocked himself. "Right in the middle of Mayfair."

Aidan came over to the bed and pulled Maddy to her feet. "We'd better learn to read all our signals better. She got mine badly mixed up."

"You got together though."

"Yes," she answered.

With Aidan's arm around her she looked at the man on the bed. He was her brother, her dearly beloved. She saw him, in a sense, for the first time, with his right to exorcise his own ambiguities and imperfections, to be loved but no longer as an extension of herself. Aidan would never let her be an extension of him.

Loyalty was bred in her but it had to take on new dimensions. She only half listened to Aidan asking and Richard answering for she heard something else more distinctly. They were all making connections—new connections of trust, perhaps. Yet they had all shown themselves remarkably trustworthy. They had all resisted the most subtle efforts to make them believe what was not true.

She had been weighing a million things in her life in the last few days, trying to assign values, and she guessed that she had sorted out some that would last her through the foreseeable future, with Aidan and for Aidan.

"You try to hold on to what makes sense," she said suddenly. "You don't let yourself be sidetracked by the things that try to confuse you. You smell the red herrings. You know there has to be an answer if you stick. So you stick. And you find it."

For the first time Richard smiled. A very small smile, not promising much but promising something.